DATING MR. RIGHT

FOUR STANDALONE ROMANTIC COMEDIES

LAUREN BLAKELY

ALSO BY LAUREN BLAKELY

Big Rock Series

Big Rock

Mister O

Well Hung

Full Package

Joy Ride

Hard Wood

One Love Series

The Sexy One

The Only One

The Hot One

The Knocked Up Plan

Come As You Are

The Heartbreakers Series

Once Upon a Real Good Time

Once Upon a Sure Thing

Once Upon a Wild Fling

Sports Romance

Most Valuable Playboy

Most Likely to Score

Lucky In Love Series

Best Laid Plans

The Feel Good Factor

Nobody Does It Better

Always Satisfied series

Satisfaction Guaranteed

Instant Gratification (September 2019)

Overnight Service (December 2019)

Standalone

Stud Finder

The V Card

Wanderlust

Part-Time Lover

The Real Deal

Unbreak My Heart

The Break-Up Album

21 Stolen Kisses

Out of Bounds

Unzipped

Birthday Suit

The Dating Proposal

Never Have I Ever

The Caught Up in Love Series

Caught Up In Us

Pretending He's Mine

Playing With Her Heart

Stars In Their Eyes Duet

My Charming Rival

My Sexy Rival

The No Regrets Series

The Thrill of It

The Start of Us

Every Second With You

The Seductive Nights Series

First Night (Julia and Clay, prequel novella)

Night After Night (Julia and Clay, book one)

After This Night (Julia and Clay, book two)

One More Night (Julia and Clay, book three)

A Wildly Seductive Night (Julia and Clay novella, book 3.5)

The Joy Delivered Duet

Nights With Him (A standalone novel about Michelle and Jack)

Forbidden Nights (A standalone novel about Nate and Casey)

The Sinful Nights Series

Sweet Sinful Nights

Sinful Desire

Sinful Longing

Sinful Love

The Fighting Fire Series

Burn For Me (Smith and Jamie)

Melt for Him (Megan and Becker)

Consumed By You (Travis and Cara)

The Jewel Series

A two-book sexy contemporary romance series

The Sapphire Affair

The Sapphire Heist

LUCKY SUIT

ABOUT

I'm breaking up with set-ups. No more "can I introduce
you to my son, nephew, grandson, the butcher, the guy
down the street who mows my lawn." Machines know
what's best, and I'll rely on the great dating algorithms
of the web to find the ideal man, thank you very much.

Soon enough, it looks like I've found him — his nickname is Lucky Suit, and he's hilarious, quick-witted and
full of heart. But when I finally get together with him in
person, I have the distinct feeling I've met him before.

Turns out there's more to our meeting than I had
thought, and when we discover what truly brought us
together, all bets are off.

1

Kristen

I'll tell Grams as soon as I see her.

I'll break the news to her and then explain why my new plan is the logical one.

First, though, I adjust the aperture on my telescope, and one of my favorite sights comes into view. The Andromeda Galaxy is such a show-off tonight, and nothing beats that billion-star galaxy. It's all yummy and triumphant in the sky, as if it's saying to the Milky Way, "I'm coming to get you in four and a half billion years."

I'm savoring the view, because the night sky rocks, when I hear footsteps.

"Tell me what?"

I startle, yank my eyes away from the telescope, and stare at my grandma, who's snuck out on the balcony we share, since her condo is right next to mine. "Were you here the whole time?"

She quirks up her lips in a *gotcha* grin. She is so good

at that. She could teach a master class in giving that grin to grown granddaughters.

"Long enough to hear you had something to tell me."

"I said that out loud?" I shove my glasses up the bridge of my nose.

She parks her hands on her hips, still fabulous in her skinny jeans at seventy-five. Dear God, may I please have her *genes*, with a capital *G*? "Yes. So . . . spill. What do you have to tell me? You car-napped my Mustang and did donuts in the 7-Eleven lot last night? You borrowed my new Louboutins without asking? Or you're selling your half of this Key Biscayne duplex because you feel guilty about the way you cramp my style?"

"One, you don't own Louboutins. You shop for shoes at Payless, and don't deny it. Two, it's a Corvette, not a Mustang. You can't trick me on that count either. And three, I can totally handle the way I cramp your style." I add a saucy finger snap for effect.

"You take after me way too much," she says, laughing. Her tone softens, the sass stripped away. "Seriously, what do you need to tell me?"

I take a deep breath. "Sit."

"Uh-oh."

I point to the table where I left my tablet. I swipe across the screen, opening it to an email I wrote earlier.

Dear Mr. O'Leary,

Please accept this letter as notice that I will be resigning from our third date, effective immediately.
Thank you for the compliments, the cup of coffee (really, that was some seriously great joe), and the chance to chat for forty-six

*minutes after we learned how to coagulate cheese. You are a fine
man and will likely prove to be an exemplary partner for a mate
someday.*

*If I can do anything to help with your transition in finding and
training my replacement, please let me know. I feel it's only right to
tell you that I am officially 100 percent done with IRL dating. So
it is with utmost honesty that I say, it's not you. It's definitely me.*

Sincerely,

Kristen Leonard

I look up to see the side-eye.

Wait. That's not the side-eye. That's the you-can't-be-serious eye.

Then it morphs into the doubled-over-in-laughter hoot.

And I maintain my best oh-so-stoic face.

"What?" I feign confusion. "Is it because I didn't spell out IRL? He'll know what it means, right? Was I too internet-y? That's totally possible." I play up my innocence, like little ole me made an etiquette faux pas. "Sometimes I get caught up in the lingo. I can just spell it out. You want me to spell it out?"

She fans her face like she can restore the oxygen she lost from her laughing fit. "Training a replacement? It was only two dates."

"Two dates too many." I straighten my shoulders. "And I thought I should be considerate in sending a breakup letter. Establish a new standard, if you will."

One eyebrow climbs. She studies me quizzically, scanning my long brown hair, my green eyes, my freckles as if she's never seen me before, then her eyes narrow. "Wait. I'm onto you. Did you simply google resignation letters?"

I let my smile spread. It's not often I can pull a fast one on her, and it's glorious. "Gotcha."

Her lips quirk up, and she wags a finger. "You little prankster. I thought for sure you were going to send this."

"Please. You know me better. I'm going to send a super-short email along the lines of *Thanks, but I feel we're not the best fit.*"

She wipes imaginary sweat from her forehead. "You had me going."

I blow on my fingernails. "I still got it. I learned from the best."

"I have taught you well, and I will now take all the credit. Also, I can't believe you didn't like Henry. Why not?"

"Look, I know your friend Betty thought we'd be great together, but I just didn't feel like he and I had anything in common. He actually *liked* the cheese-making class. I don't want to make cheese. I want it served to me. Who has time to make food from scratch when it's just as easy to order it or, gee, I dunno, *buy it?*"

"Fine, so you didn't both like making cheese. But you truly didn't connect on anything?"

I shake my head. "We didn't have a chance to learn if we did. All he talked about was the cheese. And then the coffee. Nothing more interesting. Nothing like black holes or the meaning of the universe. Or perhaps why certain cult classic TV shows aren't streaming online—like *Cupid* with Jeremy Piven, which is arguably the best show ever canceled before its time."

"And every time you mention it, I want to see it more

and more. We could try to hunt down DVDs. Did you check eBay?"

"I've tried. Believe you me, I have tried. It's harder to track down than buried treasure." I sigh. "But see, this is my point. It's such a better conversation topic than cheese."

"What about Sandy's grandson, Matthew? The one from the pickling class? He seemed like the type you could discuss anything with."

"The trouble with Matthew is the whole time during the pickling class he kept telling me about his job."

"It's normal to discuss your career with a date. I'm sure you mention your work sometimes," she says gently, as if she's talking to someone who has no clue about dating, men, and human interaction.

But I do indeed have some clue. I've been on enough dates and enough bad ones to know what I want and don't want, thank you very much. I want to leave my work as an alternative fuel scientist at the lab, and call me crazy, but some professions don't lend themselves to small talk.

"Grams. He works at a funeral home. He told me all about embalming people . . . during a *carrot pickling class*."

She tuts. "Fine, so he needs some work on social skills. Who doesn't?"

"Plus, pickled carrots? Ewww. Just eww."

"What about Sally's grandson Freddie? We set up you on the glassblowing date. That seemed fun."

I shoot her a stern look. "Glassblowing, Grams. Don't you remember what I told you? It was like a nonstop slapstick night of inappropriate jokes, and none were even funny. I love you and all of your efforts to set me up, but here's the thing: these in-person matches don't work on me. I'm evidently immune to match-making IRL."

She smiles hopefully. "Maybe you just haven't met the one yet."

I sketch air quotes. "There is no 'the one.' There are many. But the trouble is meeting men in these real-life situations has a risk-to-reward ratio that's too high." I count off on my fingers. "I've gone to singles yoga classes, and I find nothing duller than *omm*ing my way through ninety minutes of mantras. I've attended wine tastings, even though I believe it's a conspiracy to convince us the beverage is amazing when, in fact, it tastes literally like dirt, and I even signed up for ballroom dancing, but I infinitely prefer fast-paced sports on wheels. And don't even get me started on Ping-Pong lessons."

"Ping-Pong lessons are an excellent way to meet a soul mate. You do know I met your grandfather, may he rest in peace, at Ping-Pong lessons."

"That was more than fifty years ago. You were twenty-one."

"Ping-Pong was fun then, and it's fun now." She gives me a coy little smile. "After all, there's a reason your mom was born when I was only twenty-two."

I blink, pause, process. "And now Ping-Pong is officially ruined forever."

"Your mom took Ping-Pong lessons too," she says, practically taunting me. "She took them when she was twenty-four, and voilà, you were born nine months later."

I arch one brow. "I'm feeling like Ping-Pong lessons are a euphemism for something. Call me crazy."

"I'm just saying, it's fun whacking a ball back and forth."

"And the double entendres continue. Which may explain why I don't care for it, and I don't want any unexpected side effects nine months after a game."

"Fine, fine. Shall I cast a wider net, then? Ask some of my friends at poker club? Or maybe in my water aerobics class?"

I slice a hand through the air. "I love you, but no. Setups and other randomly selected in-person dates rely too much on luck and chance and happenstance. Think about it. What are the true mathematical chances I'll meet a man who is at least eighty percent compatible with me—and that's my baseline—during Ping-Pong lessons?"

She rolls her eyes. "There's a good chance."

That's the problem. I'm at the point where I want *more* than a string of dates. I want the same thing everyone wants—a spark, a sizzle, and a person. A *someone* I like being with, sharing with, spending my days with.

But that starts with common ground.

And finding common ground requires a whole new strategy.

"From here on out, it's an algorithm and an algorithm-only world." I raise my arms like a high priestess. "I believe in the church of Google. I pray at the altar of machines and put my trust in artificial intelligence." I grab my tablet and click to a dating site. "That's why I signed up for an online dating service, allowing me a wider selection of potential dates and a more systematic approach. I've already chatted with a few men. Let me show you Jared." I click on the profile of a software developer with gray eyes and a square jaw.

She shudders. "Serial killer."

"Grams."

She shakes her head. "Mark my words. Those beady eyes."

Fine, maybe Jared and his little eyes aren't the best place to start. Clicking around, I find a profile of Porter, who's new to the site and looks promising. I read his note to me out loud. *"Good evening, Kristen. It's a pleasure to make your acquaintance. I was delighted by your profile and am tickled pink to know you enjoy piano, logarithmic functions, studying new sources for alternative energy, and the companionship of a good science book."*

She stares at me like I did, in fact, steal her prized car for a late-night joy ride. "He's clearly an ax murderer."

"How on earth could you say that?"

She points at the screen. "Porter is either an ax murderer or wears ladies' underwear."

Laughing, I shake my head. "He is not."

But now the idea's been planted in my head, and I'm not too fond of it. Neither the ax murderer nor the undies.

"Let's try one more." I swipe over to Wallace. "Look, he's perfect for me. He believes in the beauty of a well-formatted spreadsheet." I flutter my hand against my chest as if it's my beating heart. "Is there anything better than the behind-the-scenes functions baked into a spreadsheet?"

"Everything. Literally everything."

I hum thoughtfully, like I don't know it drives her crazy when I go full math geek on her. "I don't know. Spreadsheets are mega hot. I think I'll write back."

She grabs my wrist, her blue eyes tinged with genuine desperation. "He could be dangerous. Why don't we use a matchmaker instead?"

"Isn't that what we already did though?"

"I mean, an official matchmaker."

"Who does that anymore? Are we in *Fiddler on the Roof*?"

"No, but that's a damn good musical."

"True. That's one thing we can agree on. But listen, I'm confident I'll find someone online who shares my interests."

"Question-asking, troublemaking, and high levels of sarcasm?"

I smile. "I also enjoy beaches, museums, and urban art, thank you very much."

And, I'd like to find that certain someone who likes the same things. Who wants to learn from me, and who I can learn from. Someone to talk to.

Someone I can share my days and nights with.

Later, I send a simpler thanks-but-no-thanks letter to Henry, and he replies with a curt *same*, only solidifying my belief that I made the right choice.

The next morning when I open the door to my condo at Grams's knock, she quirks a brow then breathes a sigh of relief. "You survived the night, I see. Now please tell me Porter didn't lock you up in a supply closet."

"No, I locked him up. Would you mind coming inside and helping me remove the duct tape from his wrists?" I deadpan.

She narrows her eyes. "You are always trying to pull a fast one."

"Because you're always trying to be faster." I shoo her away. "Go see your friends, Grams. It's Sunday Funday and you have poker club and the repo car auction."

Her expression lights up, and she rubs her palms. "I

do love seized cars. And how fabulous is your mother for finding me a new sale to check out?"

"She is most fabulous at taking an interest in our passions." My mom, I admit, is pretty freaking cool.

"If I'm lucky I can finally nab a Camaro there for Betty."

"Don't forget, if you come across a Bugatti, you better bid literally everything on it for me. Like, feel free to use my brother's rare baseball cards as collateral."

"Do you seriously think there are any Bugattis at police auctions?"

"Hope springs eternal."

She takes off, and on my way to the roller rink to work out—because skating equals killer cardio—I stop to grab a cup of coffee with my mom, updating her on Grams's ax murderer concerns.

"You know what your grams is like. Too many crime shows. Besides, you have pretty good radar when it comes to people. Just don't invite any men to your home, a back alley, a dark and deserted road, a public park, or any place with less than one hundred people. Oh, and be sure to text me before any dates with strangers so I'll know your whereabouts too."

"Oh yeah. Definitely. Want me to check in with you, too, every thirty minutes when I'm out on a date?"

Her green eyes, the same shade as mine, sparkle. "I would. Speaking of checking in, did Grams make it to the auction?"

I check my phone, nodding. "She says she's enjoying the view." I stare at her. "Your mom is a dirty bird."

2

Cameron

I like to imagine my life in montage moments.

If this were a movie, I'd get to skip the lazy slug of traffic I'm stuck in and magically appear at my destination.

Admittedly, I could have made a better effort to get to the car auction on time, but I'd been distracted when I left my South Beach hotel and spotted a pack of flamingos on the beach. Naturally, I had to take photos of them for my business partner and for my collection.

Of flamingo photos.

Yes, I have one now, because I like to snap pictures of cool things, pretty things, and weird things, and birds that stand on one leg qualify on all counts. Plus, I suspect the pic is about to become a business expense, since Lulu's unicorn avatar is flashing on my screen. In the interest of full disclosure, I did *not* set her avatar. She did.

Everyone else just gets a name. Lulu gets a magical horse, and it's blinking at me, so I swipe my thumb across the screen and chat hands-free.

"Cameron!" Lulu greets me in exclamation points.

"Lulu!"

"I have an idea. Wait for it . . ." Pretty sure I know what's coming. "Flamingo-shaped chocolate."

I nod as I tap the gas, nudging the car forward. "Go ahead. Call me brilliant. Call me a fortune-teller."

"You are, but why would I call you a fortune-teller?"

"I knew that was what you were going to say."

"And how do I know you knew that?"

I smile. "You'll just have to trust me."

"But seriously. It's a great idea, and since you're in town working on the deal . . ."

"You want me to see if the chichi hotel near the Fontainebleau would carry them?"

"It's like we share a brain."

"That, and I've been working on a deal with them for the last week."

"We should definitely make the flamingo ones for them, don't you think?"

"A better idea there has never been."

"What if we do quirky animal-shaped chocolates that are themed for the different cities where you strike distribution deals?"

"Aren't animal crackers proof that animal-shaped food is, one, awesome, and two, profitable?"

She laughs. "Okay, I've convinced you, and you've convinced me. Let's do it."

"How about you make some samples, fly down here, and come with me to meet with them in person on Monday?"

"Fine, fine, twist my arm. I'll book a ticket for tonight."

"And we'll pitch them together tomorrow."

I say goodbye and will the traffic to move faster. Eventually it does, and I make it on time to the junkyard, where I park my rental and head over to say hello to Uncle Joe, who's studying a folder of papers while leaning against an old school bus. I fist-bump the man. "Silver Fox. What's up?"

He drops the papers to his side, giving me a stern stare. "It's about time. I'm not sure I'm going to save the old beat-up Ferrari for you anymore."

My eyes bulge. "You have a Ferrari today?"

His sky-blue eyes sparkle, crinkling at the corners, well-worn from the years. "Don't you want to know."

"Seriously? Are you messing with me?"

"What would you even do with a Ferrari? You live in Manhattan. You're only here a few times a year, yet you keep coming back to the junkyard like you're really going to buy some sweet, hot sports car and drive it down the Keys."

I square my shoulders as if I've truly taken offense to his comment. "I might very well do that someday."

He scoffs. "I bet on you *not* doing that."

"A man can dream, and I dream of buying a Ferrari and cruising over the Seven Mile Bridge to the edge of the Keys."

"I'm calling your bluff."

"Why don't you step on my dreams a little more?" I stick out my polished black wing tip and crush the toe against the ground like I'm squashing a bug. "Then maybe a little further. Just dig into my dream and destroy it."

He laughs, eyeing me up and down. "When you ditch those New York suits in favor of some *Miami Vice* duds to match that whole blue-eyed-blond thing, that's when I believe you'll buy one of the cars I'm auctioning, rather than only coming here to window-shop."

I shudder. "Salmon, puce, pink, and I do not get along. Also, nice to see you too."

A smile spreads nice and wide on his face, and he yanks me in for a big hug. My mom's older brother was integral to my life growing up here in Florida. I love the guy madly. "You have no idea how fun it is to give you a hard time."

"Oh, I have a bit of an idea, since you do it all the time."

He taps the side of the bus. Usually he conducts the auction from the steps of the vehicle, megaphone in hand. "I need to review the list of goodies up for grabs. Lunch is on you today."

"Isn't it always?"

"That's what I like to hear."

I wave him off and head for the pack of car buyers, spotting a familiar face in the crowd, Jeanne. I chatted with her the last time I was here, and she's a hoot.

She's perched on an old Dodge, likely reviewing the list of items up for grabs today, with purple reading glasses low on her nose and a studious look on her weathered face. And she's wearing the least little-old-lady outfit I've ever seen—jeans and a basic black top. I imagine no elasticized waistbands of polyester have ever entered her home.

"Is this seat taken?"

She snaps up her gaze. "That depends on whether a handsome young man is going to park his butt on the hood of this car, or if some old fellow who smells like Vicks VapoRub will try to snag the coveted spot next to me."

"Definitely no Vicks VapoRub on me today, Jeanne. But young? I don't know. I'm pushing thirty-three."

She tuts. "Practically a boy-child."

I drop a kiss on her cheek, enjoying the faint scent of lilacs surrounding her. "What's shaking? I haven't seen you since that Mercury was up for grabs the other month."

She groans dramatically, clasping her cheeks. "Don't remind me. I lost out on that one, and I was dying for it."

"How many cars can you have, woman?"

She narrows her brows and wags a finger. "I have four, thank you very much. And it seems a downright sin not to have a fifth."

"Well, good thing you can make amends for that sin today."

"Indeed." She taps the list of items. "If I can snag the Camaro, I can fix it up and give it to my friend Betty."

"That's what you do with the cars?"

She smiles proudly. "It is. If I see any more of my girlfriends driving Buicks and Cadillacs, I will disown them. That's why I bid on the sports cars on their last legs then fix them up for my girls."

"Can I be your best friend when I'm seventy-five?"

She pats my leg. "Only if you play bridge, gin rummy, or poker."

I raise a hand. "All of the above."

"That so?"

I waggle my phone. "Online poker fiend at your service."

"We have lots to talk about, then."

"But first . . ." I glance at the school bus, where Joe is finishing his prep work, then whisper, "Why don't I let Joe know to give you some sugar when it comes to the Camaro?"

She clasps her hands together in prayer. "I'd say I want to win fair and square, but we all know that's a bald-faced lie, so anything he can do to grease the wheels would be fantastic. I'd be willing to pay a little more than the opening bid."

"How much?"

She gives me a number.

"Let me see what I can do for you," I say with a wink, and I return to Joe. He raises his chin, glances at me, and scrubs a hand across his silvery beard. "You again? I'm telling you, Cam, you need to take action here. Less talk, more buying."

"I'll get to it."

He sighs heavily, shaking his head. "You always did spend too much time thinking. Everything had to be analyzed, considered, weighed. Even as a kid, you debated *Should I play with the Matchbox cars or the Legos? Let me weigh the pros and cons.*"

"Those were important choices. There is nothing wrong with thinking. It happens to be my . . . second-favorite activity."

Joe laughs, pointing at me. "Good one. And I agree on the first."

"Anyway, would you do me a solid? Any chance you can make sure the Camaro goes to a certain someone?" I tip my forehead toward Jeanne.

His eyes land on her, and he whistles low. "Babe alert."

I stare at him, flustered. "Babe? Isn't she about fifteen years older than you?"

"Are you an ageist when it comes to matters of the heart?"

"No way. I just thought you liked them the same age as you."

He hums his approval. "I am omnivorous when it comes to the ladies." He gestures to Jeanne. "What'll she pay for it?"

I give him Jeanne's price, and he says he'll consider it. I return to her. "No promises, but he'll see what he can do. Should be ready to start in five minutes."

Jeanne squeezes my arm. "You're a good man. How long are you in town this time?"

"Just a few more days. I have a couple meetings, then I take off for Vegas, then Chicago."

"You need to see the Wynwood Walls while you're here."

"I heard there were some new murals." The walls in that neighborhood teem with cool graffiti art.

"They're fantastic. Also, hello, online-poker fiend. What do you say to a game before this show gets on the road?"

Smiling, I take out my phone and tap open my poker app. "What's your screen name? I'm ready to take you down."

"HotRodLover."

I sputter. "That's your handle?"

She shrugs. "It fits me."

"A little double entendre there?"

"Shame on you," she says with a smirk. "And yours?"

I smile, eyeing my getup. Joe is right. Once a suit, always a suit. "LuckySuit."

We play a round on our phones. She beats me with

an ace high, and then I even it up with a pair of kings. As the next hand is dealt, she looks my way out of the corner of her eye, asking as nonchalant as a cat padding into a library, "By the way, what ever happened to that woman you were seeing in New York?"

Briefly, I picture Isla, the clever investment banker I was seeing in Manhattan for a few months. She was pretty, witty, and chatty, all traits which attracted me, but eventually we ran out of topics to talk about. There are only so many conversations on the fluctuations in the financial markets that one man can bear listening to. Now, if she'd wanted to talk about the fine differences between rock music and indie pop, between Camus and Descartes, or between the work-to-live and the live-to-work approaches to life, we'd have shut every bar in the city down, chattering on well past the midnight hour.

"Things didn't work out with Isla. We didn't have too much in common. You know how it goes."

"You need someone who wants the same things. Who likes to think about the same things. You want someone who thinks."

"It's like you can read my mind. I believe that's the key to dating success. Opposites don't attract, in my opinion. That's for magnets. With people, like attracts like. Also, your turn."

She plays one more hand, and I win with a trio of threes. She snaps her fingers. "But let's shoot a selfie for my Instagram feed. The boy who vanquished me in online poker."

"Thirty-two, Jeanne. Thirty-two."

She waves a hand. "Still a boy."

"Also, how the heck do you have an Instagram feed?"

"I don't let anything pass me by. Just because I'm

seventy-five doesn't mean I'm not hip. I need someplace to post my cars."

She leans her head next to mine and snaps a shot of us, complete with wide, cheesy grins. "There. Jeanne and the Lucky Suit. By the way, have I mentioned that my granddaughter is single?"

This is not the first time she's mentioned her grand-daughter. "Is that so?"

"That is indeed so." She shows me a photo of a lovely brunette with the cutest glasses and a spray of freckles all over her cheeks. Her hand is wrapped around a telescope.

"She is one smart lady, never met a question she won't ask, loves to stargaze, and, wouldn't you know, she just got into online dating."

I shudder. "I will never ever do online dating."

"Really?"

I raise my right hand. "Swear to God. You don't know what you're getting into, or if they're who they say they are. And it's missing that certain *je ne sais quoi* of meeting someone in person and knowing if you have an actual connection and chemistry."

"That's a shame."

"Why is that a shame?"

She frowns. "Just think about all the women you're missing out on. All the chances you're not taking."

"Chances to have a date blow up in my face."

"Now that's not true. For instance, did you know that fifty-five percent of women say they only date men they meet online? They worry about the type of men they meet in person. The days of meeting people at bars is well over."

"Where's that stat from?"

She stares at the clear blue sky, tapping her chin. "I

think I saw it in some *Psychology Today* survey. It got me to thinking—if you don't try online dating, it's sort of like playing poker without the suit of diamonds. Think about all the hands you'd miss out on."

Soon enough the auction begins, Jeanne snags the Camaro, and I leave wondering if there's a winning hand I've yet to encounter.

Later that night, I get online.

3

Kristen

I'm a glass-half-full person. And with my glass of iced tea, I'm eager to see what awaits me online.

Tablet tucked under my arm, cool tumbler in hand, I head to my deck and park myself next to my favorite thing—my trusty telescope.

"Hi, Nicolaus." I named the scope after one of my favorite scientists. After all, Nicolaus Copernicus did discover that Earth revolved around the sun, which is kind of a big deal.

I set down the tablet and glass, thread my fingers together, and crack my knuckles. I tap on the screen. "All right, algorithms of love. Who do you have for me tonight?"

A warm breeze blows by as I click open my dating profile.

"Whoa, Nelly."

That is one full inbox.

"Maybe I'm a babe and don't know it," I mutter, then laugh.

Please, if I were a babe, I'd be well aware. I'm simply the friendly neighborhood math whiz, the girl the boys asked to be their math tutor, their science tutor, and their applied calculus tutor.

As if applied calculus is hard.

Please.

But I suppose it can be if you don't spend all day mired in the gorgeousness of math problems.

That's what dating is. One giant math variable waiting to be solved. All I have to do is figure out the way to that connection and closeness I crave. I'll crack the code to a relationship. I know I will.

I click through the chat with Porter, but as he tells me about a new article on astrophysics, I keep picturing him with ladies' panties.

I switch over to Wallace, but as we opine on spreadsheets, I wonder if he has an ax somewhere in his house.

"Shake it off, shake it off."

Maybe I need an entirely new man to chat with. Someone Grams doesn't know about yet. Someone whose image she hasn't sullied in my head.

I return to the inbox and murmur appreciatively when I spot a new name, alongside a handsome picture of a thirty-something man with a fantastic smile, blond hair, bright blue eyes, and a face that, quite simply, looks kind.

ThinkingMan is his name. I laugh then scan his profile. His mantra is *"Opposites attract" is for magnets only*. Oh yes, it is, ThinkingMan.

I click open his note.

Dear Telescoper,

As you may have surmised, I'm not a big believer in the "opposites attract" theory. But I do love theories, and from your profile, I can see you do too. While I won't pretend to be someone I'm not, and I can't claim to be conversant in all things mathematical, I do love theories, debating them, dissecting them, and deconstructing them.

Also, stargazing rules. Did you know that the Andromeda Galaxy is going to crash into the Milky Way in 4.5 billion years? Of course you do. But what do you think that collision will look like?

Best,

ThinkingMan

That's literally one of my favorite things to discuss. With a crazy grin, I reply in the chat box.

Telescoper: Greetings, ThinkingMan! I don't believe opposites attract either. In fact, there was a University of Kansas study that debunked the entire theory as it applies to relationships.

ThinkingMan: I do enjoy a good debunking. Especially since true similarities play the biggest part in pairings.

Telescoper: They do! Also, I like to think that collision will look like two stars ramming into each other, monster truck–style. But I suspect it'll be more like a river merging into an ocean.

ThinkingMan: I like that analogy. I can see that perfectly. One massive, bright, and beautiful galaxy flowing into another. I do think it'll be quite loud.

Telescoper: We're talking cover-your-eardrums loud.

ThinkingMan: Louder than the big bang?

Telescoper: I'd bet on it. By the way, did you know the Andromeda Galaxy is visible to the naked eye tonight?

ThinkingMan: I'm looking at it right now. It's always lovely on a moonless night.

Telescoper: I'm looking at Orion Nebula right now.

ThinkingMan: Don't even tell me you have some top-of-the-line NASA-style telescope. I'll be too jealous.

Telescoper: I'd hate to make you jealous, then, especially since it is an awfully big scope.

ThinkingMan: Oh no, you didn't just go there!

Telescoper: Oh yes, I did! It is huge though. After all, what I don't spend on shoes and cosmos, I spend on my telescope.

ThinkingMan: So you gave up cosmos for the cosmos.

Telescoper: Nice wordplay. Ten points to you.

ThinkingMan: And for ten points, I'll go check out the Orion Nebula too.

As we chat about the constellation and how it looks this evening, and I gaze at the night sky, I don't have to wonder if he's looking at the same stars. He *is*.

And even though it's premature to think this means anything, I'm giving my first swing at online dating a gold star.

* * *

I'll admit it.

I'm eager to talk to ThinkingMan again the next evening after I come home from work.

He's not online though, so I put aside my disappointment, burying myself in a presentation on new ways to harness wind power to make dishwashers run more efficiently.

Midway through, Grams knocks on my door, dressed in her mechanic coveralls. "I need to do some work on my Camaro. Can you babysit my Crock-Pot?"

"Isn't that the point of a Crock-Pot? It babysits itself?"

"It does, true. But dinner should be ready in a few minutes, and I want you to turn it off."

I grab my tablet and head to her place next door. When I reach the kitchen, she hands me her phone. "Take this too."

"Your phone also needs babysitting?"

She shoots me a *duh* look. "Of course it does. I'm in the middle of a game. I'm close to hitting a poker streak, but I need to get some work done on this car for Betty. Can you take over my game?"

"Sure. Do you want me to crush your opponent or just whup her butt gently like you usually do?"

She laughs. "A gentle whupping will suffice. But it's not a *she* I'm playing with."

I furrow my brow. "Who am I crushing on your behalf, then?"

"My new poker buddy. I met him at the car auction, and he's quite friendly."

"You're flirting with a poker friend?"

"Did I say I was flirting?"

"Knowing you, you're probably flirting. You said the view was nice."

"I meant the view of the cars! The junkyard was full of gorgeous, lovely cars calling out to me."

"Ah, so you were perving on the cars. Got it." I tap my temple like I'm filing away this piece of intel.

"Just. Play. The. Hands."

"What if he wants to chat?"

"Chat with him," she says breezily.

I arch a brow, adopt a spooky tone. "What if he's an ax murderer though?"

"He's not, because I met him in person."

"Question: do you think ax murderers wear name tags that identify them by profession?"

"I think you are as inquisitive today as you were when you were thirteen and I took you to the zoo and you had a gazillion questions. And do you know what I encouraged you to do then?"

I smile. "Talk to the zookeeper and ask all of them."

"Yes, so feel free to screen this man to your heart's content."

"I will definitely handle your man-friend." I wink.

She heads down to the garage, and I open her poker game, perusing the status. I see a chat window open, and I decide this is my chance to vet Grams's new guy. To find out if he's good enough for her. Just call me Inspector Kristen.

All right, LuckySuit, let's see what you've got.

4

Cameron

A pocket-size monkey swings from a tree branch.

I snap a photo of the primate then several more as he somersaults to another branch inside Monkey Jungle.

Lulu points at my subject. "You're going to tell me you want monkey-shaped chocolate next."

"Sounds brilliant. Seems my photographic pursuits are good for our business. Maybe I should work on poker chips and slot machine pictures for good luck since Las Vegas is next on the itinerary."

"And I have all the faith in the world you'll nab more deals there, and soon Lulu's Chocolates will be carried in the swankiest hotels on the Strip."

"From your mouth to the dotted-line's ears," I say as we wander through the wildlife park teeming with monkeys of all shapes and sizes. When Lulu discovered the existence of a place called Monkey Jungle near our meeting location, she begged me to take her here once business was done.

She squeezes my shoulder. "And holy smokes, did we kick butt today or what?" She high-fives me for probably the tenth time since our pitch meeting with the hotel. They loved her and her energy, but especially her chocolate. And they love the deal I'm putting together for them.

We amble over to the swimming hole, chatting as I capture a series of shots of a monkey bathing. "What a little exhibitionist."

"I don't know. He looks kind of shy. Maybe it's his first public bath," Lulu suggests.

I linger on that word.

First.

I've no plans to take a public bath, but as we walk, I keep mulling over a little thing I never thought I'd do— online dating.

It's not my style.

Not one bit.

I believe in the personal zip and zing. I believe in looking in someone's eyes. I believe in instinct. Heck, that's how Jeanne and Joe met, and they seem to have hit it off and, I suspect, will be dating any day.

I've been single long enough, and while I don't need to put a ring on anyone today or tomorrow, I'd rather get down on one knee sooner rather than later. I'd like to find the right person. The person I want to spend my time with.

"Hey, what do you think of online dating?"

Lulu squeals, grabbing my shoulders as a monkey with a raccoon mask stares at us. "Are you trying it?"

"I might be . . ."

She pounces all over my answer. "Seriously? Are you? Can I help you set up your profile?"

"Maybe I already set it up," I tease her.

"Can I see it?" She sounds like she's about to bounce off the trees.

"Wouldn't you like to see it?"

"Yes, I would. That's why I'm asking you. I want you to find your soul mate."

"And you think my soul mate is online? Hanging out somewhere on the interwebs, chilling and waiting for her man to upload his profile?"

"Yes. And when you find her, you'll know it."

"How will I know it?"

"You won't be able to stop talking to each other. You'll chat about all the things that keep you awake at night. You'll talk until the wee hours of the morning."

"Is that how things are with you and Leo these days?"

Lulu brings her finger to her lips. "Shh."

"Why are you shushing me? Leo's in New York. He can't hear you."

"I know that, but I don't want to jinx it. I'm still trying to figure it all out."

"I don't believe in jinxes."

"What do you believe in?"

"I believe in chemistry and chance when it comes to matters of the heart."

A little later, I take her to the airport and send her back to New York, letting her know I'll see her again in Manhattan. As I head to my car, I do some quick photo-shopping on my phone then send her a picture of the gawking monkey now perched on her shoulder.

She replies with a string of monkey emoticons.

I return to my hotel. Since it's June and high eighties

even in the evening, I head to the pool area, grab a lounge chair, and enjoy a little sunset breeze and people-watching. A woman in a silver bikini rides a unicycle, followed by an Elvis impersonator on stilts. A sign hangs from his neck—*Photos free, Hugs $5.*

I snap a free photo.

As the sun dips lower on the horizon, I turn to the poker app, thinking about online dating as I consider how many cards to hold and how many to fold. They're all stinkers, so I draw mostly fresh cards.

Can online dating truly lead to a soul mate? Call me skeptical. But curious too.

As I study the new cards—they aren't any better—a chat window pops up.

HotRodLover: I'm doubtful you can win a single hand.

Whoa. Jeanne is going all in on the trash talk. That's not usually her style, but I can play this way. I crack my knuckles.

LuckySuit: Is that so? Me beating you repeatedly isn't enough?

HotRodLover: Tonight, prepare to be vanquished.

I blink and scrub a hand across my jaw. What has gotten into Jeanne? She's so feisty today.

LuckySuit: Try me. Just try me.

HotRodLover: I will. There you go.

She plays her hand, winning easily. I regroup, order a beer from the poolside waiter, and we play a few more rounds. She demolishes me.

LuckySuit: Fine, fine. You're on fire tonight. I'm man enough to admit you brought your A game.

HotRodLover: Don't I always?

LuckySuit: That you do . . .

HotRodLover: Speaking of A games, what would you say is the most important thing on the path to happiness?

I crack up. I swear, this woman is a hoot.

LuckySuit: You're awfully philosophical all of a sudden. You don't want to segue into a new conversation topic? You just go for it?

HotRodLover: Please. Who needs segues? Plus, I like

philosophy. And happiness. And contemplation. So
fess up.

LuckySuit: I suppose I'd have to say kindness, fine
chocolate, friends, family, giving back, good wine and
great beer, and exotic travel.

HotRodLover: Ooh la la. You're fancy-pants in a lucky
suit.

LuckySuit: I'm not all about the jet-setting lifestyle! I
did mention family, friends, giving back.

HotRodLover: I'm all for those things too, except wine,
just for the record. Now, tell me what family means to
you . . .

I laugh at her question. It's like I'm being quizzed all of
a sudden. I take a gulp of the beer.

LuckySuit: Wait a second. It's my turn. What are your
happiness must-haves?

HotRodLover: You can't ask the same question!

LuckySuit: Why not?

HotRodLover: Rules.

LuckySuit: Rules? What rules?

HotRodLover: The rules of conversation say you must ask a new question.

As a woman in a black bikini dives into the pool, I look up, thinking of new questions and briefly wondering why my car auction and card-playing friend is so sparky tonight. A possibility tugs on my brain like a fish on a lure. I'm not sure if I'm right, but I've got a feeling, so I play out the line to see what bites.

LuckySuit: Do you believe in luck, chance, or fate?

HotRodLover: I believe fate is the creation of nonscientists. I believe luck is random happenstance and chance is simply a variable we scientists have to account for.

And that's another clue. Right there, dropped like a delicious bread crumb. I pick it up.

LuckySuit: "We" scientists?

HotRodLover: I mean "we" as in the royal "we."

LuckySuit: Now you're royal?

HotRodLover: Royally going to beat you in the next hand.

And she does just that. Then she kills me again. Each time, she's sassy. She's witty. She's firing off all sorts of one-liners, and it sure seems like my fishing line is catching something.

HotRodLover: Are you ready to admit defeat at my hand?

LuckySuit: Never surrender. I'll soldier on.

HotRodLover: Ah, I see you are relentless. Would you describe yourself as relentless?

That's an easy question to answer. All I have to do is look at the elbow grease Lulu and I put into building the concept of the stores and her line of chocolate. *Yes.*

But before I reply, I set the phone down on the wooden table next to my lounge chair. I stare up at the darkening sky, twilight falling at last. The stars will shove their way to the blanket of night soon enough.

Reminding me of something.

Something that explains why I'm liking chatting with Jeanne in a way I shouldn't be liking. Something that tells me that maybe Jeanne isn't Jeanne.

She said: "*We* scientists."

She loves to ask questions.

She's particularly fiery.

I believe I've caught something on the fishing line.

And I'm going to turn the tables on her.

LuckySuit: Absolutely. I am tenacious, determined, and focused. What about you? Oh, wait, am I allowed to ask the same questions? No, of course not. Let me rephrase. What is your favorite quality in yourself?

As the three dots flash on the screen, I can't wait to see what Not-Jeanne says.

5

Kristen

The Crock-Pot is off.

The presentation is done.

I'm winning at poker.

Grams is still tinkering in the garage.

And I'm weirdly having a blast inspecting her new man-friend. He's hilarious. And forward. And direct.

I love a good question-asker. *What is my favorite quality?*

As I drum my unpolished nails against the counter, I laugh out loud. It's the very quality that has me talking to Grams's man-friend. And it's the quality I learned from the woman herself. So it's with complete forthrightness that I answer.

HotRodLover: Inquisitiveness.

But once I send that, it's not enough. So I add a little something more.

HotRodLover: As you can see, since I've demonstrated it tonight. I possess it in buckets.

LuckySuit: Indeed you have, and it seems you have amassed quite a bucketful. Can I assume that inquisitiveness extends to the heavens above us? The stars in all their glory?

Whoa. Grams's friend is reeling me in with his talk of my favorite thing. He's getting the full seal of approval.

HotRodLover: My curiosity extends to the far reaches of the Milky Way and beyond. After all, knowing the stars helps us to know ourselves, I like to say.

LuckySuit: And why do you like to say that?

HotRodLover: They remind us of our place in the universe—how vast the universe truly is, but how we can still play valuable roles in it.

LuckySuit: Ah, is there anything better than philoso-phizing on why we're here?

HotRodLover: Nothing, nothing at all!

My face glows. He's so not a serial killer. He's perfect for me.

I mean for her.

He's perfect for her.

He's absolutely ideal for Grams. I start to tap a reply, when my own phone dings. I ignore it at first, but it chimes again, and I check it.

Mom: Hey, has Grams said anything to you about the guy she met at the car auction?

I squint at her question like it holds some clue to who the guy on the other end of the poker chat really is. I play coy to see what else Mom knows.

Kristen: No. What guy? Did she tell you anything about him?

Mom: Not enough! I'm trying to figure out if she's gone on a date with him yet. She mentioned to me that they'd chatted after she snagged the Camaro, and I was hoping it would lead to something more. :)

Kristen: Well, did you ask her?

Mom: Gee. Why didn't I think of that? ;)

Kristen: Want me to play spy for you?

Mom: Yes, go full 007.

Kristen: Anything for the woman who owns the high-rise building and lets her mom and me live here at cost.

Mom: Cost? Lady, I let you two live there at way less than cost.

Kristen: The things we do for family.

As I hit send, I spot a reply from the dating site, and a new sensation blooms inside me. *Hope.*

Hope that ThinkingMan has reached back out, because chatting with LuckySuit reminds me how much I liked talking to ThinkingMan. And that's exactly why I started a profile in the first place—to find that connection.

I click over, and there he is.

ThinkingMan: Hey, Telescoper. Are you looking at the stars again tonight? I hear Cassiopeia is going to show off and twinkle.

Telescoper: She always struts her stuff! But right now? I'm chatting. And thinking.

ThinkingMan: They are two of my favorite activities.

Telescoper: I'd like to ask what the third is, but that might be too forward. So let me ask something else—why don't you believe opposites attract?

ThinkingMan: It's a myth. A fairy tale. It's handed down from storytellers because it makes a good story.

As I type, Grams's man replies on *her* phone, and I whip my head to that screen, setting my phone down before I can write back to ThinkingMan.

I read LuckySuit's answer, trying to remember what we were last talking about in the poker app. Like a juggler, I'm tossing the conversation balls higher in the air, trying to keep my eyes on all of them. First ball— Mom and I were discussing some guy Grams met at the auction. Second ball—ThinkingMan and I are chatting about stars and opposites repelling. Third ball—Grams's friend LuckySuit and I were gabbing about . . .

We were talking about understanding how we all fit into the bigger picture. That's what his reply is about.

LuckySuit: I had a feeling you liked all things logical, scientific, and mathematical.

HotRodLover: Math is the bomb. I could do it all night and never grow tired.

LuckySuit: All night long? That's some serious numerical stamina.

I shimmy my shoulders back and forth. It's like I've consumed ten energy drinks and I'm tossing the balls in a dazzlingly high arc. I am a most excellent spy.

HotRodLover: I once entered a multiplication marathon. I won.

LuckySuit: Impressive. How long did it last?

HotRodLover: Why, I thought you'd never ask. ;) Seven hours and ten minutes. I won a calculator. Have you ever done a marathon?

LuckySuit: Yes. Do you want to ask how long it was?

HotRodLover: As a matter of fact, I think I do want to ask that. :)

I reread my last reply. And the one before. And before.

My jaw drops.

I'm falling too far out of character. I don't sound like Grams. I sound like *me* talking. Admittedly, Grams's guy is kind of cool and interesting, and he's passing all my screening tests. But I need to make sure I don't sound too much like her twenty-eight-year-old granddaughter.

Or like I'm flirting with him.

Wait. Am I flirting with this guy? Maybe a little?

It's kind of weird that I'm enjoying it.

I take a breath.

I'll just go chat with ThinkingMan for a bit, so I don't get too carried away with the charade again.

I toggle over to exit the poker app when LuckySuit replies, and my eyes pop wide.

LuckySuit: And might that be because you're actually Kristen?

Busted. The balls tumble down.

6

Cameron

Someone turns up the speakers, and Panic! at the Disco takes over the evening air poolside.

Smiling to myself, I reread the conversation. I had a feeling, and I was right.

And I have to admit, I think Jeanne might have been onto something when she dropped her anvil-size hints yesterday at the car auction about her granddaughter being single. She clearly thought we'd be a good match, and maybe she had the right idea.

Kristen is one fiery lady, and I dig that.

I dig that a hell of a lot.

But I especially like honesty.

And Kristen's showing it right now when she answers my question.

HotRodLover: Gulp.

LuckySuit: Would that be a yes?

HotRodLover: I think it's patently obvious the answer is a yes. As in yes, I'm Kristen. I'm the scientist. I'm her twenty-eight-year-old granddaughter. I'm weirdly good at poker. I also did a multiplication marathon post-college, so you can call me a geek girl, but I'll have you know I competed in Roller Derby in high school and college, so yeah, they balance each other. At least, that's what I tell myself.

LuckySuit: Let's talk about this Roller Derby. That's seriously impressive.

HotRodLover: Hold on. We *can't* keep talking. I can't talk to you like this. I was simply trying to ascertain what your intentions were with my grams!

I spit up my drink. Seriously? I stare at the question on the screen. She seriously just asked me that? I crack up as I type.

LuckySuit: My intentions with Jeanne? That's why you were working me over like a detective trying to shake down a perp?

HotRodLover: That's exactly the effect I was going for. I see it worked.

I swear I can picture the bespectacled brunette perfectly
—hands on hips, arms akimbo, chin up. Challenging me.
And yes, for the record, she looks cute in the photo my
mind just snapped. I don't need Photoshop for her.

LuckySuit: Let me get this straight. You were slinging
your litany of questions at me to determine if I'd be a
good man to date your grandma?

HotRodLover: Of course. Someone has to look out for
her. Family is important, like we were saying.

LuckySuit: Family is mega, super-duper, supremely
important.

HotRodLover: So . . . ticktock. Intentions. What are
they, mister?

She is too adorable. Too in your face. Too bold. And I like it.

LuckySuit: Let me lay things out for you. I have no
intentions with her other than friendship. And there are
many reasons for that. But one of them starts and ends
with family—my uncle is interested in her! Which also
means . . . wait for it . . . I'm not your Grams's age.

She doesn't reply right away, and as the indicator lights

bounce around, I snap a photo of the darkening sky then take in my surroundings, enjoying how different Miami is from my current home in Manhattan.

I breathe in the salt air and the warm breeze. I hear someone splashing, and I wish momentarily that this life was mine. I take the time to savor everything that's not New York City, from the pace, to the pools, to the waves, to the vast stretches of sand.

Most of all, to the mood. I do love the vibe of this tropical city. Especially now.

HotRodLover: So your uncle is the guy from the car auction?

LuckySuit: He runs it.

HotRodLover: He's not an ax murderer?

LuckySuit: Not that I'm aware of.

HotRodLover: Because you'd know if he was? He'd tell you?

LuckySuit: We're close. I'd like to think he'd divulge his profession as well as his hobbies.

HotRodLover: How do you think that sort of thing comes up? "By the way, last night I accomplished a career high of six bloody murders."

LuckySuit: Ah, so he's not just an ax murderer but a successful one? Also, it's adorable that you're screening her beaux. I suppose on behalf of Uncle Joe I should inquire if Jeanne's into him.

HotRodLover: Not to be direct, but also to be totally direct, who are you? I thought you were some man-friend of hers, and it turns out you are indeed her man-friend, but you're also not her age. You're younger. Please say you're not a teenager!

LuckySuit: I've been out of my teens for a while, but my AARP membership is still a ways off.

HotRodLover: Fine. The other question. Who exactly are you?

I glance at my shirt, my shorts, my drink. I consider the photos I take. I think about the eclectic mix of rock and indie music on my phone. I imagine my friends in New York. Who am I? I'm a lot of things.

LuckySuit: I'm the guy who believes in luck and chance. I'm the dude who plays online poker with your grandma because she's a riot and she makes me laugh, and she has ever since I met her at the car auction the other month. I'm the person who likes music and books and philosophy. I think chocolate is heaven on earth, and beer is a damn delicious beverage. And I like people. Always have. It's possible the word "gregarious" has been used to describe me. That's probably why I get along well with Jeanne. I'm outgoing, and so is she. She's also proud of you.

HotRodLover: That's quite a résumé you shared. Almost like an online dating profile. By the way, what has she said about me? Maybe that I'm an inquisitive troublemaker?

LuckySuit: Oh, I figured that out on my own. :) As for Jeanne, she brags about you, but she never mentioned Roller Derby, and now I'm dying to know all the details. Color me intrigued. What was your derby name?

HotRodLover: Calcu Lass.

LuckySuit: Was Zero Sum Dame not available? Wait. Don't answer. Calcu Lass is officially the best name ever.

HotRodLover: Why, thank you. I sure did rock a pair of high socks and skates. But enough about me. Who are you? What's your name?

LuckySuit: I'm Cameron. And in case she hasn't told you, I'm from New York, I'm in the chocolate business, and I have my sights set on a Ferrari, but I've yet to pull the trigger.

HotRodLover: I'm in the market for a Bugatti, for what it's worth.

HotRodLover: Also, gotta go.

She logs out of the app.

7

Kristen

The front door slams shut, and I sit up straight, my breath coming quickly.

Shoot. I don't want Grams to read what we were saying in her app. I will never hear the end of it if she knows how badly I flirted with her friend.

Or how *well*, I should say.

Because that was some seriously good flirting, and am I ever glad he's not *her* prospective man.

"The red beauty is nearly ready for Betty," Grams says, exhaling with relief, her work boots clomping across the floor.

My shoulders tighten, and my thumbs fly across the keyboard. "That's good." I scroll up, delete the conversation with LuckySuit, and sign out of the app. Then I grab my phone and exit the dating app, right as Grams turns the corner into the kitchen.

She's smiling.

I'm smiling too.

Wait. I need to wipe this smile off my face. I can't let on how much I enjoyed chatting with Cameron.

Or can I?

"Did you crush my friend?" she asks as she heads to the sink to wash her hands.

"I did."

"So it was an excellent night of poker and perhaps conversation?"

"We chatted a bit." The words come out stiffly.

"And?"

I'm still not sure what their connection is, so I backpedal. "I grilled him. To make sure he's good enough for you. I don't want him to stalk you or grandma-nap you."

She slaps her thigh and bursts into laughter. "He's thirty-two. He's *your* age. Not mine."

Even though he told me he wasn't too much older or too much younger, I'm glad to have the confirmation. "Oh, thank God."

"Why do you say that?" She pounces, and I suppose there's no point being coy.

I admit the truth. "Because he's quite fun and interesting and clever."

She beams, a smile that stretches to Neptune and back. "Cameron sure is, isn't he? And quite a looker, I might add."

"Really?" My voice rises. I try to erase the stupid bit of hope in it. I shouldn't be happy he's good-looking, but holy hell, I am. I almost want to ask for a photo, but that'd be gauche.

But then I remember something he said.

And I deflate.

There's no point in a photo. He lives in New York.

"He's in town for a few more days," she adds, and my heart balloons back up.

But still, with all my willpower, I resist asking to see him. He's leaving, so it's pointless. "That's great. I'm seriously behind. I need to go."

I grab my tablet and phone and skedaddle out of her place. But being next door is too close, too claustrophobic, and there are too many online men occupying too much real estate in my brain.

I text my best friend, Piper, and ask if she can finagle a late-night meeting.

* * *

By the fifth hole, I've caught Piper up on all my online dating escapades.

"This is fabulous news," Piper declares as she swings her golf club. She's a whiz at miniature golf, and I wish I could become one by osmosis.

"And why is this such a fabulous development?" I position my purple golf ball on the tee, the bright lights illuminating the course even at this late hour.

"So many of my clients these days are meeting online." Piper is something of a wedding planner, so she knows the intricacies of how couples meet and bind in holy matrimony. "Many of the online matches get engaged and married sooner, and often they seem to get along better. That's what those of us in the wedding biz call a hole in one."

I look up from the ball, club in hand. "What percentage of your clients have met online?"

She screws up the corner of her lips and glances toward the sky. Piper lives in New York, but she's in town prepping for a wedding she's working on. "Well, since you are sort of obsessed with numbers and statistics, I'll say seventy-six percent. But it's also entirely possible I might have pulled that number out of thin air."

"Well, why don't you pull it out of un-thin air? Why don't you tell me how many people really meet online?"

She pats my shoulder then gestures to the tee. "Take your turn first."

I whack the ball, watching as it rolls underneath a swinging pirate ship, landing miserably far from the hole. "You're trying to get me to mess up."

"You do an excellent job of that on your own, which is why I love playing with you."

"Someday you'll meet someone who's amazing at mini golf, and it will be unbearably difficult for you to actually have to compete," I tease.

"But that day hasn't come yet."

We walk along the green to the balls and Piper taps hers lightly, sending it to the hole, then answers my question. "Easily more than half of the weddings I do are for couples who met online. It's the most popular way people meet these days."

I hit the purple ball, and it mocks me by zipping close to the hole then doglegging away. Evil orb. "My grams thinks online dating will lead me to Jack the Ripper's door."

"Maybe it'll lead to Jack Rip-off-your-clothes-and-bang-you-against-a-door."

I wiggle my eyebrows. "A girl can dream."

With the club in her hand, she presses her palms together. "A girl can pray."

For a second, I wonder if LuckySuit is a bang-you-against-the-door kind of guy. Then I wonder where that thought came from.

Oh yeah, chatting with him.

With the guy who lives in New York, so it's pointless.

Piper flicks her chestnut hair off her shoulder. "So, tell me about these guys that you've been meeting online. I'm dying to hear."

As I tap, tap, tap to five strokes on a par two, I tell her about LuckySuit and what went down tonight. "His real name is Cameron."

"What's his last name, so we can online stalk him and see if he's Hemsworthy."

My shoulders sag. "I didn't get it."

"Ask your grams."

I shake my head. "I can't."

"Why?"

"It'd be like admitting she was right."

"Oh, well, you can't do that."

"But there's this other guy . . ."

Her eyes pop wide in avid interest, and I update her on my conversation with ThinkingMan.

"When are you going to meet him?" she asks as we stroll to the next hole.

The possibility makes my skin spark with both nerves and excitement. "Should I meet him?"

"You should meet him *and* you should meet Cameron."

"But Cameron doesn't even live here."

She shrugs happily. "It can't hurt. Just tell your grams you want to meet her friend. It's not admitting defeat. It's opening yourself up to possibility."

Funny, how earlier I was juggling one possibility. Now there are two. And both are appealing.

Especially when I find a message from one the next morning.

8

Cameron

My phone rings while I'm jogging along the beach as the pink light of dawn stretches across the sky.

"Hey, Jeanne," I say. "What's shaking?"

"Not the earth, thank heavens."

"Indeed, that's a good thing. By the way, did you hear about last night? And how I chatted with your granddaughter?"

"Only a little. Seems my Kristen deleted the conversation the two of you had, but I'm not a spy. I'm simply a little old lady who wants her granddaughter to have a nice date with a nice man."

I slow my pace, a little surprised she went for it. But then, I shouldn't be, given how she mentioned her at the auction. "You know you're not a little old lady. You're a wise, clever woman, and I bet you have some plan for me."

I can hear her smile. "You figured me out. Let's cut

to the chase. She liked you. I think you liked her. Would you like to meet her today at four p.m.? She has a shortened workday."

She names a popular spot in the Wynwood neighborhood.

I stop in my tracks, and before I can think too deeply on all the reasons to say no, I say yes.

9

Kristen

Before I leave for work, a message blinks at me.

My stomach flip-flops when I see the name.

My mind is a swirl of possibilities, switching back and forth between two men—LuckySuit and ThinkingMan.

But only one of them is asking me out.

ThinkingMan: Would you want to meet today at four p.m.?

I say yes, and I hope it doesn't come out breathlessly online. Then I ask for his name.

ThinkingMan: Mac.

Telescoper: I'm Kristen.

ThinkingMan: See you this afternoon.

I can't wait.

10

Cameron

"Look at you. All decked out for a blind date." Joe whistles at me as we chat in the lobby bar. "And you finally look like you belong here."

I arch a brow. "I beg to differ. There is not a white jacket or an ounce of pink or pastel on me." I gesture to my outfit—jeans and a navy-blue polo. Simple, casual. Fitting for a blind date.

At least, I think so. I haven't been on one since my first year out of college when my friend Mariana set me up with a preschool teacher who, it turned out, liked to snort glue.

I'll just say I'm glad I don't have kids in her school.

And Mariana is too.

Joe waves a hand dismissively. "Just kidding. You're so New York in your clothes, you're a lost cause."

"And you practically match the art deco theme here," I say, since the man looks like he can only exist in the tropics—he's gone all in on the pink shirt, for crying out loud. Yet, he's a stylish dude.

We talk some more, and I finish off my iced tea and check my watch. "I need to jet. But what about you? Are you going to get some cojones and finally let Jeanne know you've got it bad for her? I saw the way the two of you were making googly eyes at each other at the auction the other day."

"Maybe I already have . . ."

"You sly dog. Such a fast worker." I toss a twenty on the sleek silver counter of the bar. "Wait. Are you pulling my leg again?"

"Maybe I already asked her to marry me."

I clap his shoulder. "I can see I'm getting no straight answers from you."

"Have fun on your date, young turk. I'll have fun on mine with Jeanne."

I grin. "Excellent. And soon I'll be saying have fun on your honeymoon, Silver Fox."

He raises his glass in a toast. "You never know. I do have it bad for her."

"You never do know," I echo, and I take off to meet Kristen.

* * *

A happy blue alien tries to devour a yellow flower. Next to the peppy creature, a green bug chases a pink caterpillar.

I snap photo after photo of the street art, capturing the graffiti on the walls in the Wynwood neighborhood, a mecca for outdoor art with more than forty murals. I arrived early, since it's always better to be early.

Plus, taking pictures gives me something to do as I

wait. Keeps me busy. That way I don't have to focus on nerves.

Wait.

I don't feel any.

Of course I don't feel any.

Why would I? Just because I haven't been on a blind date since the glue-snorter.

I snap another shot, telling myself it'll be fine, it'll be good, and the date will simply pass the time. Nothing more can come of it, so I'll just have fun. That's all it can ever be.

"I see we both like to peer through lenses."

I lower my camera when I hear the pretty voice, turning around to see a woman in red glasses, those jeans that end at the calves, and a silky light-blue tank top. She's prettier than any blind date has ever been in the history of the universe, with chestnut locks that curl in waves over her shoulders, freckles, and a nose that's nothing short of adorable.

Hell, I stand no chance of *not* liking her. "Telescopes for you, I presume, with all your stargazing?"

For a second, her brow knits, as if I've said something odd. "Yes, I'm the Telescoper."

The designation makes me smile, so I point to myself. "The Camera-er."

She laughs. "Each gives a different perspective on the world."

"I'm a big fan of different perspectives," I add, enjoying the view of her so very much, and the conversational potential seems promising too.

"Ditto." She licks her lips, tucks a strand of hair over her ear.

I extend a hand. "I presume you're Kristen?"

She laughs lightly, like maybe she's a touch nervous

too. "Last time I checked I was." She takes my hand, and we shake. "Good to meet you, Mac."

I furrow my brow. Did she just call me Mac? But the woman is nervous, and I don't need to correct her this second. I'll remind her of my name when she's not so nervous. I gesture to the blue alien overlord. "Glad we could do this. I've been wanting to check out these murals. Did you see the one with Yoda painted every color of the rainbow?"

Her green eyes widen. They twinkle with specks of gold. "No, but I think we should see what kind of points we deserve for creative selfies. Since, you know, we gave out points for wordplay."

I rack my brain a moment, trying to remember when we assigned points for wordplay. I don't recall, but it sounds like something we'd have done, so I go with it. "Most creative selfie wins . . ." I stroke my chin as we walk. "Hmm. What's a good prize?"

She snaps her fingers. "I know. Whoever wins gets to ask five questions in a row."

"You and your questions," I say, laughing,

She shoots me a quizzical look, as if I've thrown her off.

But maybe we're both still in the nervous zone. Best to act like a comedian does when he or she is terrified of the crowd—never let them see you sweat.

I segue into another topic, hoping it eases any remaining awkwardness. "Tell me more about your interest in astronomy. Were you one of those kids who got a telescope for Christmas and it ignited a lifelong love?"

"Exactly! It was like Santa knew my true soul."

"He is one smart dude." I wink. "Sounds like your parents knew you well."

"They did." She taps her chin as we wander past a geometric painting of pink-and-blue prisms. "Actually, if memory serves, *they* gave me my first scope. They didn't want Santa getting credit for something so good."

"Now those are some seriously smart parents. What did Santa get you that year? Socks?"

"Coal," she deadpans.

"I see you've spent some time on the naughty list."

Her eyes twinkle with mischief. "Sometimes I still wind up on it."

And I'm officially a goner. This woman—I like her. I like her a hell of a lot already. This is what I'm talking about—chemistry, zip, zing. It's all about the in-person connection.

"What do you know? I've found myself on top of that list a few times." I flash her a smile, and when she grins back, I'm done for. Her smile is magical and sexy at the same time—gleaming white teeth and glossy lips that beg to be kissed.

She nudges my arm. "I can't believe you've been keeping your naughty adventures from me."

"Well, I had to save something to discuss on our date."

She laughs again. "Fess up. How did you end up on the naughty list when you were a kid?"

"Ah, you want the kid-naughty list stuff?"

"We can save the adult-naughty list conversation for a second date," she stage-whispers.

I tap my temple, as if I'm filing that away then making a note to myself. "Makes plans for second date." I sigh happily. "Okay, kid stuff. Let's see. When I was ten, I told my sister her birthday was wrong. I made her a fake birth certificate in Photoshop. I was always into taking pictures and doing cool things with them. Or cruel things. So I showed it to her, and for a few days, she believed she was a year older and kept asking why she was held back in school."

Her jaw goes slack, and her eyes widen. "You were masterfully naughty."

"That's nothing compared to her revenge."

"What did she do?"

"She knew my sweet tooth was off the charts. So she made me a pie spiked with hot sauce. Brownies with salt instead of sugar. But that's not the worst of it: she then made a batch of real chocolate cookies and put raisins in them." I pretend to sniffle and then rub fake tears off my face. "That was the worst."

Kristen's nose crinkles. "She wins the prank wars. That is fantastic." We turn the corner. "My grandma and I like to prank each other. One time she set the auto-correct options on my phone to *eggplant*, *Uranus*, and *dik-dik*, which is actually a tiny antelope."

I chuckle. "That does not surprise me in the least. She's a character. Also, tiny antelopes are adorable."

She stops in front of a giant pink mushroom. "I've told you about her?"

I narrow my eyes. Is she crazy? Then I remind myself —never let them see you sweat. And never let on you know she's sweating. "Of course you did. And nothing about her surprises me."

She shakes her head, as if she's shaking off a thought. She points to the end of the block. "Anyway, there's Yoda. Let's see how we do."

I pretend to put my arm around the green dude and snap a selfie, and then Kristen puckers up like she's going to kiss him, capturing that on her phone. We compare, and I concede. "Why am I not surprised? You definitely win. You kissing Yoda earns all the points."

She pumps a fist. "Yes, Twenty Questions time."

I hold up five fingers. "You get five questions."

She pretends to roll up her sleeves. "All right. Are you ready?"

"Hit me. I'm already warmed up from your barrage of questions last night."

She arches a brow. "I didn't think it was a barrage."

I laugh. "What exactly would you call it?"

"I didn't think I asked that many."

"That many? It was a firing squad of questions." I soften my tone as we near a mural of a flamingo. "But I didn't mind. I enjoyed them all. I was thoroughly, completely entertained to the max."

She smiles. "Me too. Our conversations have been fun."

But it does feel like we've had them separately, and I'm not sure why.

11

Kristen

I can't quite put my finger on it.

It's almost as if he's not the guy I've been chatting with on the dating site.

But he looks exactly like his online photo, which is rare. Usually they're a few years off, give or take. This guy looks precisely like his shot, almost like his picture was snapped a few days ago. Plus, Mac is so handsome, it's almost unreal.

Still, it's as if we're in parallel worlds—close, but not quite running on the same track.

So even though I've earned my five questions, and even though I should make them meaningful, getting-to-know-you ones, like *What book would you read if stranded on a desert island?*, or ones that highlight a person's sense of humor, like *If you're clean when you get out of the shower, how does a towel become dirty?*, I opt for something simpler in the hope that I can figure out if we're connecting or disconnecting.

I gesture to the mural of the flamingo. "Wouldn't it be funny if the color of our hair was a result of our diet?" He gives me a look that says I'm borderline bonkers, so I explain. "Flamingos are pink because of the pigments in their food. Carotenoids. And they eat pink food—shrimp, algae, crustaceans . . ."

He points to the saucy birds ornamenting the side of a building. "That does sound familiar. I remember learning that at some point. Now, have you ever thought about this twist—what if they ate blue fish or green birds? Would they be a different color?"

"We'd probably have emerald-green flamingos all over our mugs, license plates, and other gift shop trinkets."

His fingers grip his skull then explode. "A whole different spectrum of tchotchkes."

"It's odd, isn't it? I'm pretty sure in this flamingo-carotenoid universe, I'd be green. I'm secretly addicted to kale."

He looks at his watch. "I'm going to have to leave right now."

"Why?" I laugh.

He crosses his arms. They're quite toned, I notice. His biceps look nice and strong and would feel great wrapped around me, I bet. A zing shoots down my chest as he shakes his head. "No one is secretly addicted to kale. So you're either an alien or a robot or a celebrity on a fad diet, and I can't date any of those."

I smile. I love that he keeps saying "date." It makes me feel like we're both enjoying this in equal amounts.

I lean toward *connecting*.

I hold up my hand like I'm taking an oath. "I do. I love it. I make no bones about it."

"No one loves kale. It takes like ten years to finish one leaf."

"You've never had my roasted kale with sunflower seeds," I say, as if I'm offering a seductive treat.

"While I do like the way you talk it up, I'm sure I will never eat it." He steps closer. "Feel free to offer something else though."

"Chocolate cookies with raisins?" I purr.

He laughs. Definitely *connecting*.

"Okay, what color would your hair be?" I ask, using this chance to check him out more. The evening sun glints off his dark-blond hair, highlighting strands of gold and showing off how soft it looks. I bet it'd feel great slipping through my fingers as I kissed him.

Oh hell. Do I ever I want to kiss him. I barely know him, but what I know I like enough to want to crush my lips to his and find out if our chemistry extends to kisses.

"Blue."

"Your hair would be blue?" I ask.

"Blueberries. That's a true addiction. They're delicious, juicy, pretty, and you can down a whole basket in seconds flat. Bonus—blueberries even taste good in chocolate."

We resume our walk past the graffiti art. "You'd look cute with blue hair."

"And you'd look cute with kale-colored hair," he says, as if he's choking on the words.

"It's okay. I know someday you'll be chowing down on roasted kale and eating your words."

He cracks up then clears his throat. "But honestly, my hair would probably be brown. I do love chocolate more than nearly anything."

I hum, mulling that over. LuckySuit said he loved chocolate too. But a lot of people like chocolate. ThinkingMan can certainly love chocolate too. Besides, why am I thinking of the poker chatter from last night when I'm with this guy right now?

"In fact," he continues, "my business partner and I are going to make some flamingo-shaped chocolate."

"You're in the chocolate business?"

"Lulu's Chocolates. I handle all the business deals. Which is kind of an odd twist of fate, because back in college I was so sure I was going to be an essayist."

I laugh. "Is that even a profession anymore? Wasn't that a job back in the day when there were Federalist Papers and Alexander Hamilton and all that?"

He gives me the side-eye. "Moment of truth. Are you saying that because you know Hamilton from history or from the musical?"

I shoot him a look like I'm offended. "Hey, I know Hamilton just as well as the next person." I smirk. "Obviously, from the musical. That's pretty much how we all know him these days."

"And we all know him so well. I've seen it three times."

I furrow my brow. "Here in Miami?"

He waves in the general direction of north. "Oh no, back in New York. I try to go to Broadway shows as much as I can."

"So you're in New York a lot?" I ask, wondering if his job takes him there.

He smiles. "I am. And wouldn't it be a great place to be an essayist?"

"So why did you want to be an essayist?"

"I was a philosophy major in college, so naturally I thought I would become the next great thinker."

I nod. It's all coming together finally. "That makes sense now. Hence the ThinkingMan name."

"What?"

"ThinkingMan," I repeat, because . . . hello, isn't it obvious?

"Sure. I'd consider myself a thinking man." His answer is hesitant.

"Well, I hope so."

"Well, I am."

My mind snags on details. Philosophy. Didn't Cameron say he liked philosophy? And chocolate? While it's not unusual to like chocolate, it's certainly more unique to dig philosophy.

Disconnecting now. Definitely disconnecting.

"So that's how you picked the name ThinkingMan," I add, trying desperately to connect again.

He clears his throat. "Actually, this is probably a good time to let you know my name isn't Mac, like you said earlier."

"It's not? Why did you tell me it was?" The hair on my neck stands up. What if Grams was right? He could be an ax murderer. A serial killer.

Total disconnect.

Mayday.

Abort.

I gulp. I've been catfished. Catfished by a total creep-ozoid criminal, and I'm about to be kidnapped. I glance right, look left. A family of four strolls ahead of us. I'll run to them. Wait, no. I'll be putting their little toddler in danger. I'll dart the other way, shouting *fire!* "I forgot I have someplace to be."

I turn, ready to jet.

"Wait. No. Sorry to throw you off. I'm Cameron. Cameron Townsend. I know you know that, but you called me Mac earlier. Just wanted to make sure you remembered from our chat."

I stop.

Blink.

I'm in an alternate universe.

The parallel worlds fold into each other.

I try to breathe evenly. "You're LuckySuit?"

His lips curve into a grin. "Yeah. Who did you think I was?"

Someone else entirely.

12

Cameron

I hold my arms out wide in a question. "Who the heck is ThinkingMan?"

Her eyes are etched with confusion. Just like I'm sure mine are. She points, practically stabbing me with her finger. "You. You're ThinkingMan."

"I just told you my name. Like I told you my name last night."

"But, but, but," she sputters. "I thought ThinkingMan was your handle. I'm Telescoper. I said it when we met, and you acted like you knew it. I'm Telescoper and you're ThinkingMan. We've chatted the last few nights." Her voice intensifies, as if she's trying to make a last-ditch point in a flagging debate.

I correct her. "We chatted *last* night. When you destroyed me in poker," I say, trying to jog her memory. How does she not recall this? "Remember? You were all sassy and said you were taking me down, and then you did, winning hand after hand."

She squeezes her eyes shut, as if she's trying the good old there's-no-place-like-home technique to wish herself out of this situation. When she opens them, she says, "But we talked about Orion Nebula and wordplay. You said *points for wordplay*."

Ah, her wordplay comment makes a bit more sense now. But little else does. "Orion Nebula is a beauty, and I'd love to check it out sometime, but we never discussed that. We talked about your multiplication marathon and your Roller Derby skills as Calcu Lass. Great name still, by the way."

She sighs heavily. "Yes, I remember discussing all that with LuckySuit. But I don't understand how you're you too. How you're the other guy as well."

I laugh, confused as a tangled mess of wires. "Me neither. Well, correction. I do understand how I'm me. But I don't understand who you've been talking to."

Her face is a portrait of frustration. "It's you on the dating site. I've been talking to you."

I shake my head, slow and easy. "I'm not on any online dating sites."

She blinks, whispering in a hush, "You're not?"

"I thought about trying it out. I got online the other night. I came *this* close to setting up a profile. But I didn't pull the trigger. I was even telling my business partner, Lulu, the other day that I'd been considering it."

"You really didn't go through with it?"

I shake my head. "No. I poked around, but in the end, I didn't do it. She even offered to set up my profile. But it never felt right."

Kristen drags a hand through her hair. "You knew

about the stargazing and astronomy and asking questions though."

"Well, yeah." I'm about to add that Jeanne told me all those details, when Kristen cuts in.

"But it was *your* picture. You look just like your picture."

"My picture?" A laugh bursts from my throat. A strange *what the hell* laugh. "Someone is pretending to be me? This I need to see." I wiggle my fingers, the sign to show me the goods.

She grabs her phone, clicks on a few screens, then shoves it at me.

And there I am indeed.

Looking good.

Looking like I did on Sunday morning.

At the car auction.

The weirdness is unweirded. The confusion is de-confused. I take a deep breath. "I believe we've been catfished."

"Ya think?"

I can barely rein in a smile. "We've been pranked, Kristen." A laugh rumbles deep in my belly, moves up my chest, and spills out. I laugh harder than I've laughed in a long time. I can barely speak, and I grab her arm as if I'll topple over.

She chuckles lightly too, as if she can't quite fight it off. "Are you okay . . . whoever you are?"

I straighten, wipe the remnants of laughter away, and look her in the eye. "I'm Cameron, like I said. And it seems Jeanne was playing me, since she's the real Camera-er."

She stares at me with those wide green eyes, waiting for all the puzzle pieces to slide together. "What do you mean?"

"That picture of me on ThinkingMan's profile? Jeanne took it on Sunday. At the car auction."

Her expression transforms from perplexed, to shocked, to a new sort of awe. "Are you kidding me?"

I grab her phone, make the photo bigger, and show her where Jeanne was standing on Sunday. "There. She was right next to me. And she snapped a sneaky selfie like this." I wrap my arm around Kristen's shoulders, like Jeanne had hers around me, and mime snapping a shot.

Then I snap the photo for real. "There."

I linger for a second. Because she smells delicious. Like mangoes and pineapples. Like a tropical treat at a popsicle stand, and I would like to take a little lick of her neck. Add in a nibble on her earlobe. A kiss of her jawline.

Then, I'd kiss her lips, soft at first, then hard and properly. The kind of kiss that makes a woman swoon. That makes her melt. That's the only way a woman should ever be kissed.

But we're trying to sort out a catfishing case, so I drop my arm.

She lets out a gust of breath that tells me maybe she liked my arm around her too.

Then she laughs, full throttle, in a way that shakes her whole body to the bones. And it's incredibly sexy to watch a woman laugh so unabashedly. So shamelessly.

When she stops, she's smiling, and it's somehow brighter, richer, fuller than before.

And I still like her.

Even though I'm not sure how many conversations she's had with me, or someone else.

I show her the picture. "See? She just snipped herself out."

Kristen shakes her head in appreciation. "She is such a sneaky bird."

I smile. "And I thought I was clever with doctored birth certificates."

"A few days ago, I made her think I was going to send a formal breakup letter to the last guy she set me up with. I had her going on Saturday night, believing me."

I lift a brow. "Maybe she was trying to pull a fast one on you in retaliation?"

"Oh, she definitely wins the prank wars on this one. She's been pretending to be you and chatting with me." She shakes a fist. "I'm going to wring that dirty bird's neck when I see her again."

A knot of disappointment tightens inside me. I was hoping Kristen would be on the same page. That she was enjoying our date as much as I was. But it seems she's not sure who she's enjoyed spending time with.

"Well, maybe don't be too rough with her," I tease.

She arches a brow. "I'm going to kick her butt. And I don't mean at poker."

"You're really mad?"

She takes a deep sigh, heads to a bench at the end of the street, and plops down. I join her. "Think about it," she says. "My grandma was ThinkingMan, the guy I was chatting with. What does that make me? Some weird, strange freak who liked flirting with her . . ."

I reach for her hand, clasp it. "No, it doesn't make you anything bad at all. I suppose it simply makes her . . . clever."

She glances down at our hands. I'm holding her palm. Our fingers aren't threaded together. But still . . . she doesn't let go. She squeezes back lightly. "She really sounded like . . ."

"What did she sound like?" I try to mask my disappointment. I was honestly hoping she'd liked talking to me, not that other dude.

"She sounded like a guy who liked the same things as me. Who said all these things about opposites not attracting."

A lightbulb goes off. "Whoa. Wait a second. What did you just say?"

She drops my hand, grabs her phone, and clicks over to the conversation. "This is insanely embarrassing, but whatever. She had this whole thing about opposites not attracting."

Kristen shows me the start of the chat.

Dear Telescoper,

As you may have surmised, I'm not a big believer in the "opposites attract" theory. But I do love theories, and from your profile, I can see you do too. While I won't pretend to be someone I'm not, and I can't claim to be conversant in all things mathematical, I do love theories, debating them, dissecting them, and deconstructing them.

Also, stargazing rules. Did you know that the Andromeda Galaxy is going to crash into the Milky Way in 4.5 billion years? Of course you do. But what do you think that collision will look like?

Best,

ThinkingMan

"Damn, she's good," I say in appreciation.
    "I know."

I tap the screen. "You do realize what she did here? She used my voice. She made it sound just like me."

She tilts her head, studying me. "What do you mean?"

"At the auction, she was telling me you were single and had started online dating. I was telling her I'm not a fan of online dating because it removed chemistry and connection. And then I said I don't believe opposites attract, that I love debating all kinds of interesting topics, and that I love theories and philosophies and talking about meaningful issues. In this note, she basically parroted all the things I said."

Her jaw falls open. "Do you know what she did, then?"

"She mimicked me?"

"And she also created a perfect online persona of what I want and what I'm looking for."

And is it crazy that I want that online persona to be mine? That I want Jeanne to have stolen my traits to romance Kristen, Cyrano de Bergerac–style? "Is that so?"

She adjusts her glasses. "I don't believe opposites attract. I think they repel."

I tap my chest. "Choir. Preach it to me."

She laughs again, and if this were a real date, I'd chalk up another point. But I'm not sure what *this* is at all now. She brushes her hand lightly against my chest. "And she had you talking about all the things I like to talk about."

"Then she asked you to play her in poker against me. And when she realized we were getting along well, she set us up," I say, continuing to slide the pieces together.

Kristen scoots closer, drops her voice like we're detectives passing out clues. "That's why I don't think it was a prank, Cameron. I mean, it was. But I think she was playing matchmaker all along. She knew I only wanted to meet guys online, so she put the guy she wanted me to date online."

"And she knew I wasn't into online dating. But she wanted me to meet you. So she engineered a way for us to meet, each thinking it was exactly what we wanted— real life for me, and online for you."

Kristen scratches her head. "But she had to know we'd find out."

"Maybe she thought we wouldn't care."

"Because she figured we'd like each other and it wouldn't matter."

And I do like her. But it seems it does matter how we met. And how we didn't meet. "That must have been her grand plan."

Kristen scoffs. "That's crazy."

"Is it?"

She stares at me through her glasses. "You're fun and great and smart, and I don't know which side is up."

"I hear ya." I swallow roughly. I was hoping she'd be into me for me. And yeah, I shouldn't be bummed. I hardly know her. This is only one date.

One fun, amusing, bizarre date. One highly entertaining online chat. One moment bursting with possibilities and potential.

And that moment seems to be fizzling.

"She really hates the idea of me online dating," Kristen adds.

"And see, I'm the opposite. I don't care for online dating. Well, not until I talked to you."

She pulls away slightly to stare at me. "But was that online?"

"I think it definitely was. We were on our phones."

"Yeah," she says, the hint of a smile tugging at her

lips. But the smile fades. "It's crazy though. You live in New York. I didn't even really know who I was talking to. And it's all just a setup. It never would have worked."

"No. Never at all," I agree. She's right. But I wish she was wrong.

I sigh and figure it's best to end the date sooner rather than later.

But Kristen arches a brow, looks at me with a glint in her eyes, and I swear I see computer algorithms whirring inside her brain.

"It wouldn't. But I have a crazy idea."

13

Kristen

The first order of business is to send a note to Grams.

Me: Cameron is awesome! You were right. We're getting along so well. I can't wait to tell you everything.

Then we're off and running. We slide into his rental car, his bag with him, and drive to Miami International Airport. Once inside, we take a photo, waving with the airport sign behind us. We head all the way to security, snapping selfies as we go.

A little later, we grab our seats. More photos taken. Champagne poured. Glasses raised. "What should we toast to?" I say, a smile tipping the corners of my mouth. I'm having too much fun.

Not that there is such a thing.

Cameron stares off into the distance, as if he's thinking. For a second, it hits me—he really is ThinkingMan. He fits the bill. He talks like the man online. He seems like the man online.

How could my grandmother conjure him up so perfectly?

I blink away the thought since I don't quite know what to make of it or what to do with the wild caper we've embarked on tonight.

He meets my gaze, and those blue eyes hold mine. They shine with desire and with possibility. That look—I haven't seen it in a long time, and I like it. I like it because *I* feel it too.

He inches closer. My breath hitches from him being so near.

This is *connecting*.

"Let's toast to what comes next," he says, and the words are drenched with possibility. So much unexpected possibility that *whoosh* goes the rest of the world.

My heart flutters, and my skin sizzles as I imagine what "next" could be. Touches, kisses, sighs, moans. Butterflies, and their naughty cousins in lingerie, inhabit my chest as I clink my glass to his. "To what comes next, whatever it might be."

With my free hand, I hold up my phone and snap a photo as we move in close, cheek to cheek. I catch a faint scent of his aftershave, or maybe it's his soap. It's clean and fresh and decidedly masculine, all at once. The scent makes my stomach flip, sending a shimmy down my body on a fast track to right where I need him.

For a moment, I stop and assess the situation. That's what I do best. I apply numbers and reason. Numbers don't lie. I've felt quantifiably *more* first-date tingles with Cameron, and more intense ones too, than I have on other dates. Certainly far more than I've had on any cheese-making or carrot-pickling outings.

Obviously.

I set down my glass. He does the same.

Numbers wash away, and I let chemistry take over as I press a quick kiss to the sandpaper five-o'clock shadow stubble on his cheek. When I dust my lips to his face, I close my eyes, and a whole new zip of pleasure races across my skin, leaving a trail of sparks in its wake.

I love the scratch of his cheek.

I love the feel of his skin.

I love what it does to me.

He moves ever so slightly, and then we're looking at each other, not like two people playing a game. Not like a man and woman orchestrating a crazy idea.

We're lingering like two people who want something else.

Something we both crave. The reason we date. The reason we sift through online profiles, the reason we let our friends and family set us up, the reason we seek out another person.

For connection.

For chemistry.

And the cherry on top . . .

The prospect of a kiss.

"Kiss for the camera?" I ask. It comes out breathy, betraying all my inner longing.

I don't care.

"A kiss for the camera is necessary to pull off this caper." He makes the first move, inching closer to me. I watch him until I can't watch him anymore, until my eyes cross, and then I shut them and feel the soft whisper of his lips across mine. I gasp quietly, savoring the first touch from this man who's maybe two men, or maybe he's half of both men I liked. But even though the seesaw of LuckySuit and ThinkingMan threw me off, there's nothing confusing about the way his lips feel against mine.

Even though it's a staged kiss, it feels wholly real, especially as he lingers and I taste him on my lips.

He tastes like the one man I want now. The man I want a second date with. A second date we won't be having.

But oh, how I wish we could.

It's a good thing I'm sitting, because I'm melting from his lips brushing mine, from his scent flooding my nostrils, and from his hand cupping my cheek.

By all accounts, it's a modest kiss.

But tell that to my body.

To my body, his kiss feels dirty and delicious all over, like it could lead to hotel rooms after dark, to wrists pinned, to up-against-the-wall escapades.

To *all night long*.

We break apart.

He whispers, "Wow." All of those sparks turn into a fireworks show in my chest. Exploding, bursting. A *wow* from the barest kiss.

That may be the most unexpected part of today.

Because it's a wow for me too.

When we arrive at our destination, we scurry to a nearby palm tree, and we point upward. I know the *Welcome to Vegas* sign will be lit up and neon in our shot.

We high-five.

"We're pulling this off."

"We are seriously kind of amazing," I say.

He shoots me a look. "Kind of? We're just plain and simple amazing."

"Fine, fine. Have it your way. We're absolutely amazing."

"Are you ready for what comes next?"

I nod. "I'm absolutely ready."

"Positive? You don't want to go roller skate or lie on a blanket under the stars instead?"

I narrow my eyes. "I want to do both. Right now. All the time. But I want to do *this* too. Do you?"

"Just making sure," he says with a smile.

"Are you sure?"

Cameron laughs, and the sound makes my heart vault. Why do I like the sound of his laughter so much? I wish I knew. But I really, really like it.

"I'm very sure," he says with a smile, then loops his arm around my waist and yanks me close. "By the way, have I told you you're a whole lot of fun? Like, more fun than monkeys in a barrel?"

"But how does anyone know how much fun monkeys in a barrel really are?"

"I don't know. Has anyone ever put monkeys in a barrel and tried to have fun with them?"

"I hope not. That doesn't seem like it would be fun for the monkeys."

"And we really should be nice to monkeys," he says, then presses a kiss to my nose.

I sigh into the kiss and whisper, "I'm having fun too. More fun than if I was watching *Cupid* stream online."

He arches a brow in a question.

I wave a hand. "It's this old TV show. I keep hoping

someday it'll stream online. Let's skedaddle, and we can discuss Camus, you philosophy major, you."

His eyes twinkle. "Don't get me excited, Kristen."

"Camus gets you excited?"

"Almost as much as Descartes."

As we hop in the car, racing to our next destination, I flash back over the night. Over the kiss and the champagne, the fun and the conversations. The way we get along so weirdly well, the way we both jumped on this crazy idea.

And it wasn't an algorithm that brought us together.

It was a person.

Or maybe it was us.

* * *

At the chapel, we say hello to an Elvis impersonator and we snag a photo with him. Then he does the deed.

"I now pronounce you man and wife."

With those words, all I can think is we are getting so even they're going to need a new word for "even."

"You may kiss the bride."

"Take our picture, please, would you, Elvis?"

Elvis nods as Cameron hands him his camera.

Cameron cups my cheeks, brings my face to his, and plants the most delicious kiss on my lips.

He's gentle at first. A tender sweep of his lips. A brush against mine. Just enough for tingles to spread down my arms, leaving a trail of goosebumps in their wake.

I feel a little swoony, a little shimmery, as flutters race across my body.

Then, he kicks it up a notch. He's more insistent, a touch greedy.

And holy hell, I like greedy from him. I like it a lot. His kiss becomes demanding as his hands clasp my face, and his mouth explores mine. Tongues, lips, teeth. He kisses with an ownership, like he wants me more than he ever expected.

It's the same for me, I want to say. It's absolutely the same for me.

And I don't need to speak those words, because our bodies are talking. He tugs me closer, deepening the kiss.

The game is all the way on, and his lips devastate mine as he kisses me with a delicious intensity.

I rise on tiptoe, thread my hands around his neck, and kiss him hard. Like he's mine. Like he belongs to me tonight. And that's how this feels. Like I get to have him in this moment.

A fevered, frenzied moment punctuated by moans, and groans, and needy sighs. By kisses that can't possibly end. By a connection neither one of us wants to break because it feels so damn good.

Everywhere.

He doesn't just kiss my lips. His mouth travels along my neck, visiting the hollow of my throat. Dear god, that's spectacular. His lips on my throat send an electric charge straight through me, and I'm operating at a high voltage. He senses my reaction. I can feel his naughty smile against my skin as he kisses his way up my neck now, on a path for my ear where he nibbles on my earlobe.

And I squirm.

The good kind of squirm.

The kind where my knees are jelly from the nip of his teeth right there.

This kiss hits me all over—toes, knees, belly.

It sizzles through me, frying my brain and filling it with thoughts of where it could lead to.

Kiss me everywhere. Kiss me all over. Kiss every inch of my skin.

These thoughts run rampant in my brain, surprising me.

Stunning me with the depth of my response to him.

We hit it off instantly online, and in spite of all the mix-ups and all the puzzle pieces that didn't quite fit earlier, I feel far more connected to him in person than logic dictates I should.

Than the strange circumstances of this most bizarre date say I should.

I feel connected to him. I like him. And I don't want this to end.

But we have to disconnect.

I break the kiss, pressing a palm to his chest. "We should stop before . . ."

"Before it goes too far?" he asks.

"Yes. Exactly."

"We better. Because *far* would feel far too good."

"It would feel amazing."

* * *

Later, much later, it rains.

It seems fitting, especially since it's time to say good night. There's an empty ache in my chest.

I didn't expect to feel a hollow spot as I said goodbye to Cameron.

But the ache is real, and it hurts as I stand curbside. The rain falls, so I grab my red umbrella from my purse and open it, holding it above us.

"One more picture. Just for me," he says.

I smile faintly, and he tugs me closer and snaps a close-up. He tucks his phone away and hands me a rose.

"Where you'd find a rose?"

He wiggles an eyebrow. "I have my ways."

"No, seriously. Where did you find a rose?"

Laughing, he tells me, "Elvis gave me one to give to you."

"Well, thank you to Elvis."

Cameron runs a thumb across my jawline. "One more kiss? Just for me. No cameras."

I smile, and it seems to reach to my toes, the ends of my hair, my fingertips. "No cameras. Just us."

"Just us," he echoes as he slides a hand into my hair, brings me close, and whispers, "I'm so glad she tricked us."

"Me too."

As I hold the rose, he kisses me goodbye, and this one is bittersweet.

It's full of promise. It speaks of where those kisses could have led. To how *far* they would have gone. To the kind of nights that might have unfurled between us.

But it also tells stories that must end, since the story of our one and only date is marching toward its inevitable final line.

His lips linger on mine, the barest of touches, like he can't bear for this to end.

Same for me.

"One more," I whisper, and I'm the greedy one.

But he obliges, banding an arm around my waist, hauling me close, and planting one helluva goodbye on my lips, like the kind a sailor gives his woman when he leaves.

Then he does just that.

He leaves.

He takes off on a plane to Vegas for real this time, and I run my finger over my lips, remembering.

I go home, set the rose in a vase, and crash. I'm glad too that Grams tricked us, but I'm also not, because I wanted to believe this was something real.

14

Jeanne
   Earlier that day

As she finished up the Camaro, her phone dinged.

Wiping her hands on a red bandana, she took the device from her back pocket, clicked opened the text, and nearly squealed when she saw that Kristen and Cameron were having such a good time.

Kristen: We had a blast! We're going to spend the whole evening together since we're taking a little trip.

Jeanne had never been so pleased.

Grandmas always knew best. With seventy-five years on this earth, she was simply right.

They were so dang perfect for each other. All they

needed was somebody to bring them together, even if it took a little subterfuge. No harm, no foul. Besides, they were both so stubborn in their own ways. That was why they'd needed her—to smush them together as only she could. So what if she'd had to pretend to be Cameron for a few nights? All for a good cause, and clearly she'd made the right call.

Jeanne: I knew you'd hit it off! So thrilled. I won't say I told you so.

Kristen: You did tell me so. I have to turn my phone off now, but we'll be there in five hours and I promise to send you a barrage of photos!

Jeanne: Wait! Five hours for what—

A new message landed, and she clicked on it, opening a photo. Her eyebrows lifted. They were toasting each other on a plane? In first-class seats? What was that all about? And where were they going that took five hours to get there?

Yet they were having fun and already flying together.

Perhaps she was a better matchmaker than she'd thought.

With a satisfied grin, she went inside and prepped for her own date, grateful that Joe had had the gumption to call her up after the auction. They'd already gone to a classic car show the other afternoon in South Beach, and they'd had such a fantastic time that he'd asked her to go to the racetrack tonight. That man was a handsome devil, and she was delighted that he didn't seem to care that she was fifteen years older. Did that make her a cougar?

She roared at herself in the mirror and brandished her cougar claws.

"So be it."

She swiped on mascara, some lipstick, and headed to the racetrack.

* * *

Her phone dinged once more as a hot green sports car cheetahed its way around the track.

"You waiting for a girlfriend to give you an out?" Joe teased.

She patted his leg. "Puh-leaze. If I didn't like you, I'd tell you to your face."

He flashed an *I'm waiting* smile. "Well?"

"You know I like you. The question is, how much do I like you?" She smiled.

"I'd like to know how much."

"So would I," she said flirtily then grabbed her phone. "Let me see if it's Kristen."

She flinched when the photo loaded. What were they doing *there*? Were they truly in Sin City?

"Look," she whispered, showing him the picture of Kristen and Cameron beneath the Vegas sign.

"Seems they like each other. Just wanted to get away for a night in Vegas."

She knew Cameron had been heading to Vegas for work, but had Kristen gone along with him? Didn't she have to work the next day? Vegas was . . . well, a five-hour flight.

Her phone buzzed once more.

She startled.

And what was this? Elvis? And a chapel?

She froze. Kristen, her sweet, darling, clever Kristen, had fallen so quickly she'd eloped in Las Vegas?

She shook her head, like there was water in her ears. "She was supposed to look at urban art, get a cup of coffee, and maybe have a kiss," she blurted out.

Joe cocked his head, stared at her quizzically. "Come again?"

She shoved the screen at him, showing him the string of texts. "They eloped! They ran off to Vegas and got married."

Joe nearly spat out his drink as he gawked at the photos. "What is up with kids today?"

"I knew they'd like each other, but this seems a touch extreme."

"Just a little."

But at the same time, she couldn't help but pat herself on the back. It was extreme, but sometimes you just knew.

15

Cameron

As the hotel executive shares his ideas for where he wants to introduce a Lulu's Chocolates cart in the lobby of The Luxe, a newer Vegas resort, I listen furiously, giving him my undivided attention as best I can.

Because my attention these last twenty-four hours has definitely been divided.

I'm here, chatting in the lobby of this hotel.

But my mind is back in Miami, running around the city as we pranked Kristen's grandma, making her think we loved our setup so much we'd run off to Vegas to tie the knot.

Photoshop for the win.

Right now, I'm hardly thinking of photo-doctoring software that made us look like we were in a first-class cabin or under the famous Vegas sign. Nor am I thinking of poker chip–themed chocolate, though I know I should be.

I'm remembering that last kiss.

An airport kiss.

The kind that makes you want more. That makes you wish one person wasn't going one way and the other person going another.

Heck, I'd love to be hopping on a plane to Miami again tonight, rather than returning to New York.

When the meeting ends and the exec tells me the deal looks good, I ought to be happy.

Too bad when I hop on a plane that evening, I'm not exactly jumping for joy.

As I fly over the country, I tell myself it was only one date. "Get over it, man."

16

The next morning, I hit the roller rink at the crack of dawn, working out on my skates. I have an hour before I need to be at work, so I skate then return home, ready to shower.

Grams pounces on me the second I walk through the doorway.

She grabs my wrist. "Tell me everything."

I clasp my hand to my chest, flutter my eyelids, and do my best starry-eyed impression. "Oh, it was magical, and I'm in love."

Her eyes twinkle. "You are?"

The funny thing is . . . it doesn't feel far from possible. Not today, but down the road. Maybe in a few months, I could honestly see myself falling for Cameron.

That's what doesn't add up.

It's illogical. It's irrational. It's ridiculous.

But it's also why my heart weighs heavy.

Grams stares at me, studying my hands. "Where's your ring?"

I walk inside, drop my bag on the couch, set my phone on the table, and turn around. I don't have the energy to keep up the prank anymore. I've pulled her leg and gotten her goat. It was a blast, and yet, I'm sadder than I want to be.

I shrug. "It was a joke. We didn't go to Vegas to get married. We spent the evening running around Miami, taking pictures under palm trees and then photoshopping them to look like the Vegas sign, an airplane, and so on."

Her eyes bulge. "What? How?"

"We bought champagne and glasses, went to the monorail, parked ourselves in the seats, and toasted on it." I don't add that we kissed on the monorail and that it was some kind of magic that didn't need an ounce of retouching in a photo. "Then Cameron photoshopped it to look like we were on an airplane."

Her jaw clangs to the floor, cash register–style. "You didn't." Her tone says she can't believe she's been had, yet she's also wildly impressed.

"We did. Then we snagged the Elvis impersonator on the beach and went to a chapel here on South Beach, and we pretended to get married."

"Why did you do all that?"

I park my hands on my hips. "Why did you catfish me?"

She tuts. "I would hardly call it catfishing."

"I would precisely call it catfishing."

She squares her shoulders. "I knew he was right for you."

"He's great," I say, unable to mask the affection I feel

for him. "But I want to make my own choices. You had me going. You made me feel . . . a little foolish."

Her expression falters, and she frowns. "But you liked him."

"Yeah, I did. And I do. But I also felt kind of stupid when I learned it had all been a ruse."

"It wasn't all a ruse. You loved chatting with him during poker, didn't you?"

I squeeze her arm. "I did, but don't you see? I want to make my own choices, and I want you to respect them."

She exhales, nods, and licks her lips. "I'm sorry if I overstepped. I just thought he was a good man for you, and it was the only way I could get you to meet him. Plus, I didn't make anything up—everything I told you was from conversations I'd had with the real Cameron over poker. So technically, you were talking to him—just through me."

"Like you're a medium now?"

She snaps her fingers and grins. "Exactly. I was channeling him."

"You made it sound so real," I say, a little sad. "I wished it'd been him. And I wish you'd just asked me to go on a blind date."

"After the pickle embalmer and the cheesy cheese-maker, you'd have said no."

"True," I admit.

"Aren't you glad you said yes?"

I scoff. "I didn't say yes!"

"You can't think of ThinkingMan as me. He was Cameron. It was all him."

I shoot her a skeptical look. "It was actually all you."

"Technically, but the profile was based on him, and when I knew the two of you actually liked each other after your poker chat, I figured it was fine to set you up on a date."

"What if I hadn't liked him playing poker?"

"But I knew you would."

"What if I hadn't?" I press.

"Well . . . I don't know," she admits. Then she reaches out, wraps her arms around me. "I'm sorry if I was out of line. I want you to be happy and to find the right person. I thought you'd like him."

I rest my cheek against her shoulder, catching a glimpse of the rose in the vase, fading after only one night, as roses do. "I did like him, and you were right. But here's the trouble." I separate and meet her eyes. "He's gone. He doesn't live here."

She waves a hand dismissively. "What's distance when love's involved?"

"One, we're not involved. Two, it's a big thing. Three—"

"Just get on a plane and see him."

I raise a finger. "Do not secretly book me on a flight. Or him. Do you understand?"

She laughs and raises her right hand. "I promise."

Then she mutters, "For now."

* * *

Later that night, I open my tablet, and I'm tempted to check out the online dating site. But the guy I want to talk to isn't there.

The next morning I find a text on my phone.

It's not from ThinkingMan.

It's not from LuckySuit.

It's from Cameron.

17

Cameron

I'm not over it.

Not over her.

Not interested in getting over the best date of my life.

I have no agenda, no notion of what's next. But as I walk down Sixth Avenue, the warm summer breeze wrapping around me, I picture the montage of moments I want right now.

And all the shots are of Kristen.

I decide to stop thinking about texting her . . . and text her.

Cameron: Question. When you skated, were you as feared on the rink as you were at the blackboard?

Kristen: But of course. I made opponents cower.

Cameron: I'm not in the least bit surprised. Do you still skate, and when you do, do you wear those socks that go to your knees?

Kristen: You mean . . . wait for it . . . knee-high socks?

Cameron: Yes, those.

Kristen: I do. Got a thing for knee-high socks?

Cameron: Interesting question. I'd love to find out. It would be helpful if you could send me a photo of you in full skater regalia, knee-high socks and all, and then I could answer you honestly.

Kristen: All in the name of research and learning, of course?

Cameron: Of course.

I wait patiently, threading through the morning crowds as I head to meet Lulu. Two blocks later, my phone buzzes and I'm rewarded with a photo.

There. Is. A. God.

It's a picture of Kristen—legs only. She's wearing white knee-high socks with purple stripes.

Those legs in those socks. Kill me now.

Cameron: Do you realize you make socks sexy?

Kristen: Why, thank you. You make . . . polo shirts sexy?

Cameron: You remembered what I wore. :)

Kristen: Or maybe I'm looking at some of the photos we took . . .

Okay, now I have a city-wide grin stealing the real estate on my face.

Cameron: Maybe I've been doing that too. Good thing we took so many pictures.

Kristen: Do you have a favorite?

I stop at the crosswalk, click over to my photo folder, and find the last shot. The one I snapped at the airport. I didn't photoshop this picture. It's just us, before the night ended. I send it to her.

Kristen: Ah, I like that one too. And now I have one more to look at.

Cameron: I might have looked at it a few times already.

Kristen: I'm catching up to you right now on that tally. By the way, what are you doing today?

Cameron: Contemplating chocolate, business deals, and how to grow wings and/or learn to Apparate.

Kristen: And what exactly would you do if you could Apparate? Inquiring minds want to know.

Cameron: Take you out, pretend we were at the Taj Mahal, maybe add Mt. Everest or a Buddhist temple behind us, possibly even the Leaning Tower of Pisa. Or we could visit Monkey Jungle and mock up a picture of us in a barrel testing the baseline of fun. Other options —take you to a bookstore and get lost in books on philosophy. Go to a concert and decide whether indie is better than pop, or just debate it all night long. Take you to a roller rink and watch you skate in those knee socks, then take them off . . .

Kristen: Where do I sign up?

Cameron: You good with all that?

Kristen: With every single thing. But you know what I like most?

Cameron: Do tell.

Kristen: Talking to you as you.

Cameron: I like that too. More than I want to.

But now I have to end the conversation. I say goodbye and head into the shop, feeling both better and worse.

18

Kristen

I text him the next afternoon.

Kristen: Today my hair is purple. I ate eggplant for lunch.

Cameron: I've got an eggplant right here for you.

Kristen: *facepalm*

Cameron: You did walk right into that.

Kristen: I did. I totally did.

* * *

That night he texts me.

Cameron: By the way, I've been meaning to ask about the Orion Nebula.

Kristen: IS THIS YOU?

Cameron: YES. WHY?

Kristen: You know this is how I was catfished! The Orion Nebula was the bait.

Cameron: I'll prove it's me.

I wait, and his picture appears on my phone. His face. Then his . . . feet? Is he actually wearing . . .?

Kristen: Are you wearing Crocs?

Cameron: Yes.

Kristen: Why would you show me Crocs and, more importantly, why would you wear them?

Cameron: To answer the latter, they're comfortable. To answer the former, to prove it's me.

Kristen: That proves this is you?

Cameron: It proves I'm me because if I were someone

else impersonating me, he'd never humble himself by showing Crocs. I'm showing you who I really am.

Kristen: A Croc wearer?

Cameron: Yes, do you still like me?

My smile is contagious. They're grinning in the next county, and they caught it from me.

Kristen: Yes. But for the love of pi and the golden ratio, please never show them to me in person so I don't have to bleach my eyeballs. Deal?

Cameron: Deal. Especially the in-person part.

Kristen: Also, is it so obvious l like you that you knew even Crocs wouldn't ruin it?

Cameron: Call me crazy, but I like obvious on this count. In fact, I like it a lot. And I like you—a whole helluva lot.

Kristen: Same . . . it's totally the same. Even in Crocs.

Cameron: Now, back to the Orion Nebula. Evidently, the first me, who wasn't me but rather based on me, talked to you about it. But I wanted to look at it tonight, and since you're a stargazer, I was hoping you could give me some guidance.

And my heart goes thud. It falls to the floor, beating for him, like a silly, lust-struck fool.

Kristen: I'd love to. But it's easier to talk it through on the phone.

Three seconds later, my phone rings.

"What a cheap excuse to get me to call," he teases.

"But it worked."

"I'm easy like that."

I go to the deck, stare at the night sky, and tell him how to find the constellation. When we're done searching millions of miles away, we talk about music and our friends. I learn about Lulu, and I tell him about Piper, and the ache in my chest grows.

But so do the feelings.

They balloon.

"What are we doing?" I ask.

He sighs, a little sadly. "I don't know. I shouldn't be calling you like this. It makes everything harder."

"I know. Talking to you till all hours makes it harder."

"It makes me wish I were there."

I lean back in the chair, closing my eyes. "What would you do if you were?"

"Kiss you." His voice is a sexy rumble.

I hum. "Where?"

"Your lips, the hollow of your throat, your earlobe, where you like to be nipped."

I shiver. "Do I like to have my earlobe nibbled on?"

"Oh, you absolutely do. And I'd kiss you for hours."

"I'd squirm for hours," I whisper.

"I like all the sounds you make when I kiss you. I'd like to know what other sounds you make."

Flames. I go up in flames. "I suspect you'd be cataloguing a whole lot of noises."

A soft chuckle comes from his end of the line, followed by a sexy sigh. "I'd like to kiss you everywhere, Kristen."

And I die. From the visual my brain helpfully assembled. From the shiver that rushed down my belly thanks to that image. And from the possibility of his mouth exploring me everywhere.

When we hang up, I'm lonelier than when we started.

* * *

It would have been smarter to stop, but we don't. We keep going over the next few weeks, as I work and see my friends, as he works and travels more for business.

Every night, we talk.

Every day, we text.

Every time, the math geek in me craves a solution. We are one side of the equation, and I don't know how to solve for x with all these miles between us.

I long to know what's on the other side of the equal sign.

One day when I return home from work, I find a package waiting outside my door. Bending, I pick up the padded manila envelope. Once inside my condo, I slide open the envelope, then I shriek.

Oops.

I'd shrieked so loudly that Grams opens her door seconds later.

"Cockroach, gator, or dragonfly?"

Laughing, I shake my head, clutching the package to my chest. "Neither. It's *Cupid*. DVDs of *Cupid*."

"That Jeremy Piven show? Who sent them?"

I can't wipe the dopey grin off my face. "Cameron."

She arches a brow knowingly. "Told you so."

I pluck the card from inside, opening it. *"Where there's a will, there's a way. I tracked these down for you. I hope you enjoy every single second of them. The only thing better would be if you were wearing knee-high socks and curled up next to me on the couch."*

He's right.

That's the only thing that would make this better.

The next day I send him a gift. One that lets him know how much I like this one.

19

Cameron

"What do you think? Great name for the new line?"

I blink up at Lulu. Shoot. What did she just tell me was her idea for the new line of chocolate?

I was too busy replaying last night's conversation with Kristen, when we listed all the things we could do in either a Ferrari or a Bugatti.

News flash—driving *wasn't* that high up.

Still, Lulu deserves an answer, and since she's aces at names, I take a wild guess that she's devised a fantastic one. "Brilliant name," I say, leaning against the counter in the shop. It's quiet right now. There's a lull in the afternoon traffic.

She shoots me a thumbs-up. "Fantastic. Toe Jam Chocolate it will be."

I adopt a straight face, though I cringe inside. "Excellent."

She shakes her head. "You are so busted."

"Please, I knew you were putting me on."

She shakes her head, poking my chest. "You. Did. Not."

"Did. So."

"You lie."

I shrug. "Fine, you caught me. I was drifting into Daydream Land."

"You've been spending a lot of time in Daydream Land since your Miami trip with Kristen."

I sigh heavily. "I know, I know."

"Heck, that weekend you guys took me to the Hamptons, you were texting her the whole time," she says, reminding me of the trip a bunch of us took Lulu on when she needed to sort out the complexities of her love life. I *might* have been talking to Kristen a whole lot that weekend. And the next week. And the next one. And telling Lulu about her. "Which makes me wonder," she adds, "why are you still here?"

"Where should I be?"

Lulu stares sharply. "Not here."

I shake my head. "I'm not doing something crazy."

"Why not? That's what love is."

"This was just a date."

"It seems like it's one fantastic date that's lasted a few weeks."

I shrug in admission. She's not wrong. "Maybe it has."

"And that brings me to my big question."

I furrow my brow. "What's that?"

Before she can answer, though, the bell above the door rings and the UPS man strides in, handing her a package.

"Must be supplies," I say, offhand.

Lulu smirks as she looks at the front of the envelope. "Supplies for you, lover boy."

My interest is piqued. "And why do you say that?" I ask as the man leaves.

Lulu holds a package behind her back. "This might as well be tied with a satin bow."

"But it's not tied with a satin bow, is it?"

She waves it above her head. "It's from your mystery woman. *Kristen.*"

My heart thumps faster. I have no clue what Kristen sent me, but whatever it is, I want it. I reach for the package.

Lulu holds it behind her back.

I roll my eyes. "We are not playing these games."

"Promise me something."

"What on earth do you want me to promise you?"

She tells me what she wants me to do after I open the package. I laugh in disbelief. "That's bonkers."

She shakes her head. "That's what you told me to do when I was all up in the air over Leo."

I shoot her a quizzical look. "I don't believe *that* is exactly what I told you to do."

She waves her hand. "Just open it."

Like a college prospect waiting for a scholarship notice, I rip open the envelope. And then I grin. Then the grin grows entirely naughty when I read Kristen's note.

Lulu shakes a finger at me. "Don't break your promise."

I don't plan to. I definitely don't plan to.

* * *

Later that night, Jeanne texts me with an idea. But I've beaten her to it.

Cameron: I'm on it already.

20

Kristen

Piper taps her chin, considering the lavender dress at the bridal shop. "So much lavender. I wish the bride chose yellow. I have twenty lavender dresses."

I arch a brow. "Twenty? That seems an exaggeration."

"Come to Manhattan. Check out my closet. I solemnly swear I have twenty."

As Piper holds up the dress to her mirrored reflection, I sink onto the plush pink chair. "I'll stow away in your bag. Go back with you."

She spins around, looking at me with sharp eyes. "You could."

I scoff. "Hide out in your bag?"

"No, goofball. Come back to New York with me."

"You're right. I don't need a job. I'll leave my condo. And my family."

"For. The. Weekend."

"Then what happens after the weekend?"

She taps her chin. "Gee, I don't know. Fly up another weekend if it works out."

"Just jet back and forth from Miami to New York?"

She nods exaggeratedly. "Yeah. It's called a long-distance relationship. You do know it's been done before? You didn't invent this scenario of falling for a guy who lives a thousand miles away."

"Thanks for clarifying. I thought I had."

"It's the modern age. People meet online. They date long-distance. They make it work."

"That's a lot to make work."

"And how many evenings have you been talking or texting him on the phone all night long?"

I cast my gaze down, grumbling, "The last several."

"And I bet some of those texts weren't entirely safe for work."

"I did not sext him. I didn't send any nudes."

She arches a brow.

I huff. "I sent him a shot of my legs. But it was a tasteful shot."

"I've no doubt he wants a taste of you."

I laugh, but my stomach is swooping, because I'd like that too. "Maybe," I say noncommittally.

She laughs, sets the dress on a hook, and strides over to me. She lifts my chin. "You could get on a plane to New York and surprise him, and I bet he'd be ecstatic."

"That seems a little presumptuous."

"Then ask him if you should . . . *presume*."

But can I ask him that? Are we at that point? I marinate on Piper's advice as I return home, then I reread the last few nights of texts.

I stare at the photo from our date.

I close my eyes and I recall how it felt.

I open my eyes and grab my phone.

Kristen: This might be crazy, but is there any chance you might want company this weekend? Or want to be my company this weekend?

He doesn't reply.

And I do my best to pretend that doesn't equal one very sad Kristen.

21

Cameron

The car rumbles through the streets, and in the back seat, I reread my most recent chat with Jeanne.

Jeanne: I'm keeping her busy till you arrive.

Cameron: You're a good woman.

Jeanne: Also, I beat you with a full house.

Cameron: It's about time.

Jeanne: Hey, be nice to the little old lady.

Cameron: As if that description fits you at all.

Ten minutes later, my Uber arrives at my destination. I thank the driver and bound up the steps, then knock on the door.

For a second, maybe more, I wonder if this is crazy. If I've gone insane, presumptuous, and all kinds of soft inside for trying to pull off this surprise.

Maybe I have.

Maybe I'm jumping off the nutty end of the diving board.

Maybe that's okay.

Hope rises in me. A big balloon of it. Nerves expand too, relentlessly.

But what's life without a big chance now and then? After all, she's worth the risk.

Kristen opens the door. Her chestnut hair is piled high in a messy bun, her glasses are sliding down her nose, and her cute pink skirt makes me think very bad things.

Her expression, though, is priceless.

It's hope meets wild hope.

It's *Is this really happening?*

It matches mine.

She parts her lips to speak, but I go first.

I smack my forehead. "My bad. You texted me and asked if I wanted company this weekend. Figured I'd tell you in person that the answer is yes."

She grabs my shirt collar and yanks me inside, crushing my lips with hers in a hot, searing kiss. The door isn't even closed, and I don't care. She's on fire, devouring me, and I want to be burned. My head is a haze, and my body is rocketing to five-alarm levels.

Then she lets go.

"Whoa. Why'd you stop kissing me? You should do

more of that. Never stop kissing me. Also, do it all night long."

She laughs and kicks the door closed. "All night long can be arranged. Also, this is perfect timing. My grams just left about ten seconds ago."

"Good. I told her to keep you occupied till I arrived."

"Wait. Did she engineer this too?"

I laugh as I slide my hands around her waist. "No, but she did tell me she thought I ought to get my butt down here. And I told her I was already on it."

She ropes her arms around my neck. "Good. Because I like your butt. Also, you had me worried."

I tug her closer. "Woman, when you send me a deck of cards with a note that says *Want to play strip poker sometime?* I am on it. I booked the next flight out of town to see you. Yes, maybe Lulu made me promise that I would get on a plane to see you, but it was all I could think about anyway."

She brushes a kiss to my lips. "Maybe let's stop talking and thinking and texting, and start doing."

That I can do.

I thread a hand in her hair and seal my mouth to hers. It's one of those slow burn kisses, the kind that takes its time, heats you up, and warms you inside and out.

But it's only slow burn for so long.

Because weeks of longing? Late-night phone calls? Flirty, dirty texts? And the kisses we shared on that first date?

The time for slow burn is over after one delicious minute of soft, gentle, open-mouthed kisses.

My circuits go haywire, and my desire rockets to sky high.

I grab her ass, lift her up, help her hook her legs around my hips, and then I carry her to the couch.

"Kiss you everywhere?" I ask, arching a brow, as I tug off my shirt. "I believe that was one of your requests?"

Her eyes blaze, and she's stripping at the speed of light too. There goes the shirt, the bra, and hallelujah. My brain is officially fried because . . . breasts.

"Yes, but right now, I kind of need something else."

"And what would that be?"

She sits up, reaches for my jeans, and makes her intentions clear. "You naked, fucking me."

What do you know? Her intentions match mine. "I aim to deliver on all your needs."

A few more seconds, and that pretty pink skirt pools on the floor, and my boxer briefs join it.

She reaches for my shoulders, bringing me close, whispering, "Hi."

"Hi," I say, as I roll on a condom.

"Also, please get inside me right now."

I laugh. "You are so damn direct and it's a hell of a turn on."

Her eyebrows wiggle as her hand darts down, clasping my erection. "I can tell. You are definitely turned on."

I groan from the red-hot pleasure, the wild thrill of her hands on me. Then, I groan from the sheer perfection of sliding inside her. This woman I adore. The woman I crave. And the woman I want badly.

She lets out the sexiest sigh in the entire galaxy as I fill her, and then she arches up into me, gripping, moving, owning her pleasure.

She's so alluring, so unabashed as she seeks the right

angle, the right friction, then as she asks me to go a little faster, a little harder.

"You're going to kill me," I murmur.

"Don't die till we both come," she says, then she shudders, and lets loose a fantastic *oh god*.

My own lust shoots higher, but I stave off my finish, needing to get her there first. Needing to make sure she's all good.

And judging from her trembles and moans, from the flush in her cheeks, the part of her lips, she is way more than good.

So am I, in fact.

I'm great as her body quakes, tightening around me, then she cries out.

And that's my cue to follow her there.

We lay sated and spent, but not for long. There is kissing, and cuddling, and showering.

And then there is even more kissing.

Everywhere.

I give her what she wants, and she gives in to the sensations, wrapping her legs around me, moaning, groaning, and calling my name as I bring her there again with my mouth.

That's what we do all weekend.

And we make plans to do it again the next one.

I'm not going to let a little thing like distance stand in the way any longer. Life is complicated; love is even more so.

But there is nearly always a solution.

This is ours—we're making it work.

EPILOGUE

Cameron

A few months later

My phone flashes with a text. The words "hot tip" scream at me.

Jeanne: Word on the street is there's a seized red Ferrari coming up for auction this weekend. Maybe if you're nice to Joe, he'll hold it for you.

Cameron: Maybe if *you're* nice to Joe, he'll hold it for me.

Jeanne: I'm always good to Joe.

I roll my eyes and show the phone to Kristen, who's

curled up with me on her couch on a lazy Sunday morning.

"Once a dirty bird, always a dirty bird," she says, then tugs me in for another kiss.

I'm all too happy to oblige. But there are things to discuss, so I pull back, running my finger down her nose.

"So . . . should I get the car?"

She lifts a brow. "What would you do with a car in Manhattan?"

It's an excellent question.

I tap my chin as if deep in thought. "True. When you come see me in New York, we spend most of our time in bed anyway."

She swats me. "Not true. We went to museums, and we walked across the Brooklyn Bridge, and we went to the planetarium, and we took pictures in front of Lincoln Center's fountain. But we were never in a car, Cameron."

I run my fingers through her hair. "We were never in a car in Manhattan . . ." I trail off, waiting for her to get my meaning.

"Right. And . . .?"

"But we do have to use a car . . . *here*."

She sits up straighter. "What are you saying? That you want a Ferrari to drive around in when you come visit me every other weekend?"

I shrug, grinning.

"Fine. But that seems like quite an indulgence."

I crack up. "I like indulgences. You're an indulgence." I press a kiss to her forehead then cup her cheek, meeting her gaze. "But what if it wasn't an indulgence? What if, say, I needed a car to get around town more regularly?"

Her face freezes. She goes stock-still, then she speaks in a whisper. "What are you saying?"

I can't resist toying with her logical head. "Work the problem, Kristen. What's the solution to the long-distance problem of you and me that would merit a car?"

She licks her lips. "Are you saying . . .?"

I shake my head. "I'm not saying. I'm asking. Or rather, I'd like you to ask me."

I smile, waiting.

She takes a deep breath, trembling. "Do you want to move in with me?"

"Why, I thought you'd never ask."

"But what about your job?"

"I'll run it from here. I'll make it work. I'll go back to New York from time to time. But I can't take being away from you a minute longer."

"Have I ever told you I love you more than the Milky Way?"

Her smile is wider than the galaxy.

Kristen

I'm cheering Cameron on at the auction. So is Grams. She's by Joe's side, since she's been helping him run it from time to time over the last few months.

"They're a perfect couple," I say to my mom, who wanted to come along today.

My mom hums, nodding like she has a secret up her sleeve. "They truly are. It's like they were meant to be together."

"What's that smile all about?"

She tilts her head and grins wider. "Just that I had a feeling all along about them."

"Right, that's what you said."

She clasps her hand to her chest. "Oh, allow me to clarify. It was more than a feeling."

"What are you saying?"

"I'm saying I might have a little cupid in me too." She blows on her red fingernails.

"Is that so?"

She shimmies her shoulders. "I met him at the hairdresser's and had a hunch he was right for her. So I started sending her to the auctions."

I squeeze her arm. "You little matchmaker, you."

She winks. "And you know what that means, my little genius?"

"No, what does it mean?"

"Put two and two together."

"Four?" I ask playfully.

She shakes her head. "It means I'm essentially responsible for you and Cameron getting together too. If I hadn't sent Grams here, she'd never have met him. And now look at the two of you."

I look at my guy as he bids and wins a hot red sports car. Then I turn to my mom. "I do owe you a thank-you. You knew exactly what I needed to be happy."

She shakes her head. "No, I simply hoped you'd find someone you loved. Someone you connected with. You made all that happiness happen on your own."

That afternoon, Cameron drives off the lot in his new sports car, looking all kinds of sexy behind the wheel, with me in the passenger seat.

He drapes an arm over my shoulder. "What do you say we go drive around my new city and buy towels or shaving cream or whatever it is that I'll need to live here?"

"Nothing says sexy like driving your hot new Ferrari to Bed Bath & Beyond."

We drive off into the sunset.

Two wild cards that turned into a perfect match.

If you enjoyed this novella and want to read Lulu's love story, please check out *Birthday Suit*. Piper's love story will be told in *Never Have I Ever*, coming soon.

ONCE UPON A
RED-HOT KISS

A Heartbreakers novella

ABOUT

A man needs to stay far away from falling into bed with his best friend.

Even if she's sexy as sin, sweet as candy, and damn near irresistible every single day.

But not only are Macy and I best friends, we're also complete opposites. She's perky, upbeat, outgoing and I'm . . . how shall we say . . . a little bit broody.

Then, she reveals something to me that just might lead me to revise all my rules on friends in bed...

1

Kirby

Red.

Everywhere I see red. Hearts, flowers, balloons, candy, cards, ribbons, streamers, and Cupid.

That dumbass angel is everywhere. On windows. Winking from billboards. Shooting arrows in stores.

As I head down Eighth Avenue to the rehearsal studio, it's as if New York City has grown red octopus arms, and every storefront spews pink paper hearts, teddy bears, and every possible valentine decoration, topped off with candy-bearing, soul-sucking sayings like *Be Mine, Let's Kiss,* and the worst one of all—*Soul Mate*—mocking the non–soul mate seekers of the world.

It's three days from that wretched holiday, and I would give up a free lifetime supply of pale ale if I could escape from pink, red, and white New York for the next few days.

Wait. That's crazy. I'd never give up a lifetime supply of good brew.

It's not that I hate Valentine's Day. It's that, well, Valentine's Day hates me.

I'm cursed.

Truly.

Bianca Sweetwater hexed me in fifth grade when I sent her a white rose instead of the red one she wanted. In my defense . . .

I WAS ELEVEN.

I thought a white rose was just fine.

She said a white rose meant friendship, and I said friendship was good, and she said everyone knew friends couldn't fall in love, and I said I was eleven and didn't want to fall in love, and she raised both arms high above her head, mimed shooting lightning at me, and declared I was cursed to fall in love with a friend who'd never love me back, just as I'd done to Bianca.

I shudder at the memory as I push open the door into the building, leaving the cold air behind. I say hi to Pete, who mans the desk here.

"How's it going? Did you see the game last night?"

"I did. And now I'm just counting down the days till Valentine's."

I refrain from rolling my eyes. Is there anyone in this city who doesn't give a shit about the holiday? I want to talk hockey, not hearts.

"The Mrs. is big on V Day, I take it?"

His smile spreads from cheek to jowly cheek. "She is and so am I. I like to go all out for my woman. Italian dinner. Gourmet chocolate. Flowers."

"You do all that? For a greeting card holiday?"

He puffs out his chest. "Damn straight. Only folks with a black heart don't like it."

Laughing, I add, "Guess I have a black heart."

"Ah, I don't believe that, Kirby."

"Oh, it's definitely black. Just like my ink." I hold out my arm, even though he can't see the swirls of tattoos under my Henley.

"Someday you'll tattoo a woman's name in a heart under that whole badass tough guy exterior."

"Ha. I sing songs on YouTube with my sister. I don't have a badass exterior."

"Take away the songs, and you're one hundred percent tough guy, won't let anyone in."

I wave him off, even though he's kind of right. "See you later," I say as I head to the elevator.

Look, I don't believe in white magic or black magic. But curses? There's something to them. Some people just have bad luck.

I've been lucky in some aspects of love. *Cough, cough.* The ladies like me and I like the ladies.

But love? That's been a tough nut to crack, and every year Valentine's Day reminds me.

Starting way back when.

For instance, in seventh grade I failed a math test on the holiday because the teacher claimed I hadn't turned it in. Bianca's handiwork? Perhaps.

In ninth grade, I'd brought a white teddy bear for my friend Madison Greenbray, a cute, nerdy girl. But when I reached for it in my locker to give to her at lunch, the bear was missing. He turned up later that day in the dumpster.

As a senior, when all the girls were swooning over the Valentine's Day flower exchange, I decided to try again. I ordered a red flower for Lily Van Tassel, a good friend at the time.

Only one problem.

Everyone else liked Lily Van Tassel. Everyone sent her red roses. Including Chuck Zorax, the wrestler who was seven feet tall and built from redwood trees. When he found out I'd sent a rose to Lily—even though I was one of so very many who did—he introduced my nose to his fist.

As the doors to the elevator open, I step in, rubbing my palm against my nose. Yup, still have the crook in it to prove that sliding out of the friend zone doesn't work.

Learned my lesson.

Love and friendship don't mix.

That's why I haven't tried to level up in the friendship game with a certain someone.

Sexy, snarky, lively Macy who thinks Valentine's Day is fabulous.

Macy thinks everything is fabulous.

She's the most upbeat person I know. She's the Tigger to my Eeyore.

I reach the sixth floor and head into the rehearsal space to find her standing on a stepladder, pinning a pink paper heart to the wall. For a moment, I savor the view. She's wearing tight jeans, black boots, and a pink sweater that's as snug as a sweater on a babe should be.

So snug I want to pull it off and discover what's underneath. To get my hands all over her lush, trim figure.

But I can't linger there too long or it'll be tent time.

Can't let on I have dirty, filthy fantasies about the sweet, perky blonde.

Especially since she's one of my best friends. I stare at the decorations, since they're a boner killer, and in seconds, that does the trick. Tent's all packed up. "Wow. Did Hallmark lose its lunch in here?"

She shoots me a smile that stretches from her green

eyes to Queens and back, chiding me as she reaches for a red paper heart from a bag on the top step. "Don't be silly. This is way more than Hallmark is capable of. This is what happens when Target meets Pinterest meets Etsy and I assemble the most beautiful valentine decorations in the world."

"And please tell me why our rehearsal space has turned into a valentine fiesta?"

She spreads her arms out wide. "Because Valentine's Day is wonderful. It's romantic and full of all the best things in life—like hearts and hope and love and *red*. Have I mentioned I love the color red?"

My eyes drift to the decorations. "You didn't have to mention it."

"Don't be such a naysayer. The rehearsal space has never looked better."

I furrow my brow. "You can't be serious about all this."

She climbs down the ladder, parks a hand on one hip. Her pouty pink lips curve into a grin, and I'd like to kiss that smile off her face. Kiss it and make her moan against my mouth, sigh against my body.

But yeah, there's that little matter of friendship, and that big curse about how friends can't be lovers.

"I'm deadly serious. I never joke about valentine decorations. Just look at all the yumminess here." With her blonde ponytail bouncing, she strolls over to the grand piano, where my sister and I will perform our patented duets for a new YouTube series. Macy taps a glass bowl crammed with red candy.

"I love cinnamon." She dips her hand into the bowl, plucks out a red cinnamon heart, and pops it in her mouth. Her eyes seem to light up. They twinkle. They sparkle, and her lips do all sorts of interesting things, as she sucks on that red heart. My dick does all sorts of things too, perking up and taking notice.

Down, boy.

"Do you like cinnamon?" There's something new in her voice. It's a little sultry, a bit naughty.

And matters south of the border are liking that voice. I step behind the piano. God bless erection shields.

"Love cinnamon." I bet she tastes like cinnamon. I bet the taste would drive me wild on her tongue.

"Then you won't object when the Zimmerman Duo's new series is Valentine's themed."

I press my hands together in a plaintive plea. "Please, for the love of all that is holy—like spring training, the power play in hockey, and any and every Rolling Stones tune—tell me you're joking."

She clasps her hands over mine. "You are twenty-seven and a total curmudgeon."

"So that's a maybe that you're joking?"

She squeezes my hands tighter, and this isn't such a bad turn of events. Macy touching me? I'll take it.

She shakes her head. "I know you hate it, but it's going to be fine. YouTube is giving you and Ally some great placement, and since I'm sort of your manager, I also appointed myself chief decorator. That means you're going to suck it up, like a big boy."

I sigh in an exaggerated fashion. I can't stay irked at Macy. "Well, since it's YouTube . . ."

YouTube has been good to my sister and me since we formed our duo and began producing online videos of popular mash-ups of songs. Since we were young kids, Ally and I have duetted, and I sure don't mind the way the income supplements my day job at an ad agency.

"Fine," I admit grudgingly. "As long as I don't have to wear a red shirt or cupid hat."

"Oh please, I know you hate all that. We're only going to make you sing." She takes a beat, shoots me a playful look, and says, "Vrooge."

"What?"

"You're Vrooge. Valentine Scrooge."

"Wow, that is harsh."

She shrugs coyly. "If the name fits."

"Then I will wear it with pride, because I am definitely Valentine Scrooge."

The trouble is this Vrooge is crazy for a woman he can't have.

No wonder Vrooges are grumpy fuckers.

2

Macy

"He has no *voliday* spirit. Simply none," I tell my friend Olivia as I sort through a display rack at Eden.

"Some men are like that," she says nonchalantly, checking out a drawerful of satin underthings at the lingerie boutique in Chelsea. She loves to shop here, and she's positively addicted to sexy garments. Maybe because her husband is addicted to them too, and when he sees her in them, he can't resist, or so she tells me. It's not as if I've witnessed his helplessness before her feminine charms.

She likes his inability to resist.

"But Kirby's truly against the entire concept." I frown, stopping my hunt for just the right sexy number. "It kind of makes me sad."

Olivia tuts. "Macy, Valentine's Day is not everything."

"Of course it's not *everything*. But it is a fun, festive holiday. I love it. I always have."

Olivia shoots me a look with cool blue eyes. "True. You used to make me valentine cards back in school."

"I baked you cookies too. And I tied bows around them. Admit it. I'm all kinds of awesome."

"You are thoroughly fabulous. But so what if he doesn't like it? It's just another day."

I shake my head vigorously. "Oh no, it's not."

"Look, I do enjoy flowers from my hubby, and a big old basket of chocolate, but it's a made-up day."

I shake my head, correcting, "It's a day made up of fabulousness. Plus, I don't think you so much enjoy the chocolate. You work off the chocolate horizontally, don't you?"

She shrugs knowingly. "Perhaps we do."

"So if your hubs likes it, and Ally's friend Miller likes it, I can convince Kirby to like it."

"I don't know. From what you tell me, Kirby's a committed bachelor and a committed Valentine's Day hater."

My optimism rules the day though. "That's just because he hasn't experienced the Macy Valentine Treatment. I know deep down that Kirby Zimmerman could learn to love it."

Olivia continues her hunt, assessing lacy boy shorts now. "Ooh, these are hot," she says, showing me a black pair with a tiny white bow.

I pant like a dog. "So sexy."

"I'm getting them."

"See! You try to deny you like Valentine's Day, and here you are buying lingerie to seduce your husband."

She smiles like she has a dirty little secret. "Studies

show that sex on Valentine's Day can deliver multiple orgasms."

I grab the black panties from her. "Gimme them. I want more than one O. Wait, I haven't even had a single O from a man in a while. I won't be greedy. I'll happily take just one, thank you very much." I give her back the panties, and return to the rack of red teddies, sexy tanks, and racy bras that boost boobs in ways that will drive a man wild.

I'd like to drive Kirby wild.

There's only one issue.

Yes, he's my good friend Ally's brother, but Ally doesn't care about that. She's not one of those "don't touch my brother" girls.

The issue with Kirby is our friendship.

He's committed to it, and has said as much many times over. I love him madly as a friend too, and working with him, planning the videos, then grabbing a cup of coffee and gabbing about everything and nothing has been fantastic. He's funny, smart, and has just enough of a grump in him that my happy side wants to convert him to the light.

I'm completely devoted to our friendship.

But I'm devoted to something else as well.

Having more of that man. Every time I look into those bright blue eyes, each time I take in the cut of his jaw with his perma five o'clock stubble, or catch a glimpse of his ink-covered arms, I want more than friendship.

That's why when I find the pretty red bra, demi-cup and deliciously lacy, I decide it's perfect for seduction. "This will do the trick."

"Ooh la la," Olivia says approvingly. She touches her finger to her tongue and then the air, making a sizzling sound. "But if you really like him, and I know you do, aren't you better off asking him out on a regular date? Like, maybe during literally any other time of year?"

"What's so wrong with trying for Valentine's Day?"

She laughs. "You're fighting a losing battle. If you truly want that man, you should seduce him at a hockey game."

I stick out my tongue. "I disagree. If he can't fall for the spirit of Valentine's Day, then he's not the man for me."

"It's that simple? V Day or bust?"

"Look, Valentine's Day has been good to me. I won a scholarship for college on Valentine's Day, I landed my first good makeup artist job on this day, and I saw Wicked on Valentine's Day and went backstage to meet the woman who does the green makeup. It's my good luck day."

She rolls her eyes. "Every day is your good luck day."

"True. I'm kind of made of sunshine. But that's also why Valentine's Day has to be it. I don't need to convert the man, but I also don't want to get involved with a man who's stubborn and set in his ways. Think of it as the perfect litmus test. If he bends a little, I'll know he has an open mind and heart. It'll be a sign that he won't shut me down. I don't want to clash too much with him, so I need to know we can both bend a little."

Olivia drops her hand over mine, stopping me. Her expression turns serious. "If you're trying to win his heart, you shouldn't use lingerie."

I pout. "Why not?"

"How will you know it's not simply sex if you're seducing him *with* sex?"

I consider her question. Olivia has always been the quizzical, logical one. But even though I lead with enthusiasm—hello, I *was* a former cheerleader—I have plenty of logic in ye olde brain too.

And sometimes the way to a man's heart starts with his other parts. "But maybe that is the way to his heart."

And if it is, I wouldn't mind finding out.

All I need is a sign from him.

3

From the texts of Ally & Miller

Ally: Did you hear the news?

Miller: There's a new edition of Bananagrams? I am so on it. I'm going to the store right now. I can't wait to spell "diphthong."

Ally: You are ridiculous! As if that's why I'm messaging you.

Miller: Then spill the beans. Why are you messaging me if it's not for something as epic as a new board game? We could even play dirty words.

Ally: It's amazing that you're actually an adult.

Miller: Don't say that word. Makes me feel like an old man.

Ally: Anyway, I was texting to tell you something fun. Drumroll . . . Kirby and I are doing a series of special videos. For . . . guess what?

Miller: Winter solstice? The next lunar eclipse? When the Yankees finally turn good again?

Ally: Please. That last one will never happen.

Miller: Don't remind me. I know too well.

Ally: We're doing a Valentine's series of music videos.

Miller: Hell yeah! That's only one of my favorite holidays.

Ally: Every holiday is your favorite holiday.

Miller: I believe in holidays. What can I say?

Ally: You are definitely a holiday lover.

Miller: Holidays, vacations, time off. I adore them all.

Ally: Time off from what?

Ally: Collecting royalties from all the hit songs you recorded from your hot boy-band days?

Miller: I've recorded plenty too in my hot man days.

Ally: True, some would say you're still a heartthrob.

Miller: Once a heartthrob, always a heartthrob.

Ally: You said 'throb.'

Miller: I've got a throb right here for ya, baby. :)

Ally: You're too much. Anyway, it's ironic because my brother is a total Vrooge. That's what Macy calls him.

Miller: The Kirbster is a total Vrooge. And what's the point in being that? V Day is all about love and sexy times and getting into the groove. That makes it a very good day.

Ally: I should have known you'd find a way to make it seem naughty.

Miller: Naughty valentines are the best kind.

Ally: Why do I even try to have a serious conversation with you?

Miller: Sorry, was this serious? My serious temperature taker said it was most decidedly not serious.

Ally: Like every conversation with you. :)

Miller: That's why you love me.

Ally: I do love you. You're the best friend a gal could have.

* * *

Miller: Note to self—remember that. Best friend a gal could have.

Miller: New note to self—there is nothing more that's going to happen with Ally. Ever.

Miller: New new note to self—no matter how much you want to change her mind.

* * *

From the texts of Kirby & Macy

Kirby: I wanted you to know I've recovered.

Kirby: Well, mostly recovered.

Kirby: Actually, I'm still suffering.

Macy: What happened? Are you okay?

Kirby: From the way you and my sister subjected me to hearts and teddy bears at rehearsal today.

Macy: What sort of recovery has been required? Was it lots of chest-thumping, Tarzan-ing, and other exceedingly masculine pursuits?

Kirby: Mostly it was pizza and beer. That's often the answer. To all of life's questions. And to pretty much everything.

Macy: *rolling eyes hard* Also, I refuse to believe you hated it that much.

Kirby: I'm trying to understand how you like it so much. Why? Tell me why.

Macy: Are you seriously asking me?

Kirby: Yeah. I'm trying to understand the obsession that women seem to have with it.

Macy: Are you grouping me in with all women?

Kirby: Not in a bad way, but women seem to dig it.

Macy: I don't think it's only women who dig this holiday. There are a lot of guys who do too.

Kirby: Name one.

Macy: From what Ally tells me, Miller likes it.

Kirby: Miller likes everything. He's the world's happiest person.

Macy: And what's so wrong with liking it? Or being happy?

Kirby: It's a social construct.

Macy: Lots of things are social constructs. And we still like them. The obsession with hockey could be considered a social construct.

Kirby: Whoa. That's hitting below the belt.

Macy: Did it hurt?

Kirby: Nah. It's just other things below the belt are more fun.

Macy: From Valentine's Day to social constructs to naughty jokes . . .

Kirby: I'm down with that direction.

Macy: I bet you are.

Kirby: Bet it all.

Macy: Anyway, I'll get to the bottom of your disdain. :)

Kirby: How? Will you torture me with teddy bears and candy hearts?

Macy: I have my ways.

Kirby: I'd like to know what these ways are.

Macy: Would you, now?

Kirby: Yes, I very much would like to know your ways . . . especially if they go in certain directions . . .

Macy: I know what direction you mean . . .

4

Kirby

Tugging my jacket tighter, I turn the corner as the wind whips along the city street.

New York City is a cold mistress in winter, and this February she's punishing all her residents. I'm done with work at the agency for the day—a task complicated by the minefield of secret cupid shenanigans at the office, but I've masterfully avoided all the valentine exchanges. It was a short day for me, and we're recording the videos this evening. Then I'll be done with this stupid holiday.

And on the day itself? Since Valentine's Day is a Saturday, I'll while away the day with sports and success-fully avoid the love fiesta.

As I pass a jewelry store, I snap my gaze away from its obnoxious window signs about sweethearts and rings.

Besides, the whole complicated situation with Macy is another slap in the face. Even if I pursued something with her like I want to, it would surely go belly up. Bianca's curse would prove true.

The woman I want is simply off-limits. She's my friend, and friendships like this don't come around often. I don't want to chance messing it up.

Knowing my luck, I'd lose her as a friend.

I grab the door for Doctor Insomnia's Coffee and Tea Emporium and head into my regular haunt. Escape at last—I can completely avoid the holiday in this store. The guy who owns the shop doesn't have a single valentine decoration in the window.

God bless him.

I stride up to the counter and give a fist bump to Tommy, the owner. We catch up on music, and he gives me the names of some cool bands he's been listening to. As I order a latte, he asks how things have been going at the ad agency.

"Working on a cool new ad campaign for a video game maker, and the client loved it. So I can't complain about work." That's a place where I have good luck. "All's well with you?"

"Life is always good," he says as he makes a latte for a woman wearing a raspberry knit hat.

I glance around. "This shop is just what I need. I'm so glad you didn't give into the madness of the holiday."

The woman clears her throat, cutting in. "Could I trouble you to do one of those little latte hearts?"

"Absolutely," Tommy says with a smile as he works his latte art magic.

I roll my eyes.

Tommy hands her the drink, and she grabs a seat. "You need to get over your hatred for Valentine's Day," he says, his tone a little stern.

"Why's that?"

"Because someday you're going to be with a nice woman, and she's going to expect you to bring her flowers, roses, chocolate, everything."

"Hopefully I'll meet a nice woman who doesn't expect those things."

"I don't think you need to *meet* a nice woman." His growly, rough voice rumbles through his shop.

I furrow my brow. "Wait. You just said I needed to meet someone. I'm confused. Do I or don't I?"

He presses his palms on the counter, his eyes intensely serious. "I think you already met her."

"What are you talking about?"

He laughs and wipes the washcloth along the counter. "You met her a few years ago. Every time you come in here with Macy, you look at her like she's the one you want to give flowers to, like she's the one who deserves all the roses in the world, like she's the one, like she's the fucking *one*," he says, emphasizing the last word.

I blink. I do? But inside, I'm wondering how did he nail it? Is it that obvious? I deny. "You're crazy. I don't want to give her flowers. We're friends. Therefore, it'll never work."

Hello? Doesn't he understand that I was cursed by a wicked witch?

Tommy shakes his head, laughing. "You young kids."

I'm not that young. "I'm twenty-seven."

"That's young."

"What are you saying I should do, O wise one?"

He drops the cloth, stares at me. "I'm saying that maybe you ought to get over your hatred of this holiday. And maybe you ought to get over all the reasons you're not pursuing anything with the lovely blonde. Want to know why?"

"Tell me why."

His eyes pin me with an intensity I rarely see in them. "Because she's a sweetheart. A fun, great, kind, and caring woman. If you don't see all that, trust me— another man will."

I bristle, ten tons of annoyance landing on my shoulders. "How can you be so sure?"

He scoffs. "Some things you just know. Someone will appreciate her." He reaches across the counter to poke me. "The question is—will it be you?"

I heave a sigh. "But what if it doesn't work out?"

He answers with an eye roll. "What do you want to drink, kid?"

"Latte, please."

He softens his tone as he sets to work on the beverage. "I know you think you're full of bad luck or some such nonsense. But luck is what you make. So make your own luck. Let the woman know you've got it bad for her."

His points are prodding at my skull, making me reflect on my own reluctance. Still, the obstacles seem too big. "And what about the fact that she's best friends with my sister? What about the fact that *we're* friends?"

He waves a hand dismissively. "Complications, whatever. You can sort it all out. In the old days, you know what the complications used to be? A soldier was going off to war and he wasn't going to see his woman for four years. That was a motherfucking complication. You've got a minor problem."

"I feel like that's not really a fair analogy," I say, deadpan-style.

"No, it's not a fair analogy, and that's my point. You don't have a big problem. You have a little, itty-bitty, teeny problem, and little problems can be solved easily.

Man up. Are you man enough to give the woman you want a latte with a heart on it?"

I shudder.

But somewhere inside, I know he's asking the right questions.

And I need to find answers.

He slides me the latte he made for me, adding a heart.

I rein in my desire to roll my eyes.

I drink it, and as I do, I contemplate. I marinate. I wonder.

Fuck it.

I order two to go.

5

Macy

As I dust eye shadow on Ally's lids, she hums a few lines from the song they're recording shortly.

"Oh, I like that one," I tell her. I take a step back and appraise my handiwork. "You look amazing when you're made-up, but just the right amount of made-up."

Ally smiles at me. "You always have to make sure I look like the quintessential good girl for the vids."

I giggle in an over-the-top way, like her wholesomeness is the best-kept secret. "And we know you're really *not* a good girl."

"I'm good enough." She trails off with a wink.

Kirby and Ally have been racking up YouTube views since they launched their brother-and-sister act a few years ago, singing sweet and lovely songs like "Amazing Grace" meets "Somewhere Over The Rainbow." Beautiful, rich, heartfelt songs in the kind of duet style that makes everyone want to go full *Glee*.

I remove a lip liner from my makeup bag. "I love your good girl persona. And I know it's *mostly* true. But then again, I know plenty of other secret details about you."

"Like what?" She lifts a skeptical brow as I uncap the liner.

"Like how much you're into Miller."

Her jaw drops. "I'm not into Miller. We're just best friends."

I pretend to be taken aback. "What am I? Chopped liver?"

"Best guy friend," she clarifies. "And I'm not into him like that."

I outline her lips. "You were when you first met him. Don't try to deny it."

"I'm not denying it, but we made a decision to focus on the friendship. Sort of like you and Kirby."

Laughing, I shake my head. "Your brother and I never *made* that decision. We fell into it."

She smacks my free arm playfully. "Well, fall out of it. Go get your man."

"Are you seriously telling me to go after your brother?"

She nods. "Uh, yeah. Can you please, please, please put him out of his misery?" Ally clasps her hand to her mouth, careful to avoid touching her freshly glossed lips. "Oops. Didn't mean to be so pushy. But seriously, you guys are destined to be together."

Hope flutters through me. I'm so damn lucky she's behind me on this count. But just to be sure, I ask, "Are you absolutely positive you don't hate the idea of me being with your brother?"

She rolls her eyes. "I'm positive."

"And you think we're meant to be?"

"Like peanut butter and chocolate. I don't care about the whole *opposites attract* thing. There's enough in your core and his core that's the same."

I reflect on her words, thinking back to our texts last night, to all our texts, all our conversations, our easy way of talking. Even when we don't see eye to eye, Kirby and I seem to enjoy not seeing eye to eye.

"You might be right," I muse.

"Maybe give him the kick in the pants he needs, then?"

A huge smile crosses my lips. "I'd like to. I'm ready to try." I tap her shoulder with a makeup brush. "Also, I still think you should go for it with Miller."

She whips her head back and forth. "No, we're only going to be friends. I don't want to lose him."

I grab a tube of mascara. "Are you saying friends can't be lovers?"

She taps her chest. "For me. I'm saying it for me."

"Ah, so you admit you have a thing for him?" I say like I've caught her red-handed as I finish a quick touch-up on her lashes.

She growls. "Nope. Did not."

"That's okay. I know you did."

"But none of that matters, Macy. The night we met we agreed to be only friends."

I stare at the ceiling as if I'm deep in thought, then back at my friend. "Did you actually agree, or did you decide in your head you wanted him to be your friend so you would never be tempted to pursue anything more and get hurt?"

She hisses. "She-devil. You're always trying to trip me up on semantics."

I flash a smile. "It's easy to do because you keep

holding yourself to this arbitrary, silly, ridiculous rule. The very same one you want me to break."

"It's a rule that makes sense."

After I put the finishing touches on her cheeks, I tuck my brushes away and zip up my makeup bag. "I think you should break your rule."

Kirby strolls into the rehearsal space. "What rule should she break?"

I flash him a smile. "I think she and Miller should go for it. Do you agree?"

"And risk the friendship?" Kirby arches a brow.

"Yes."

"Is that worth the risk?"

Confidently, I raise my chin, even though nerves flitter everywhere inside me. "Some things are worth the risk."

"Like what?"

"Like telling someone how you feel," I say, and I want to say more. To tell him everything. That I want him to be mine.

Every year since I've known him, I've hoped he'd be mine.

I want him to tell me he's been crazy about me too, then pin me against the wall and kiss the breath out of me. He could take my wrists in his hands, slide them up the wall, and plant kisses all over my neck. He could bring his lips to mine and devour me. And I'd let him. I would let him devour me because that's what I want more than anything. I want red-hot kisses and dirty, naughty sex with my friend. I want my friend to become my lover.

But right now, I want the latte he hands me. One for me, and one for his sister.

"Best brother ever," Ally declares as she takes off the lid.

When I remove the lid from my cup, mine has a heart drawn in foam. Mine's the *only* one with a heart on it.

And the presence of it makes the organ in my chest somersault.

We spend the next few hours recording their video series. Every now and then when they're at the keyboard, when he's singing, I swear he looks at me.

Like maybe he's seeing me in a different way.

Like maybe that heart means something more.

6

Kirby

Are you man enough to give the woman you love a latte with a heart on it?

Hell yeah. I manned all the way up.

But that's not enough.

Once we're done with the videos and Ally leaves, the night is still young.

"That latte was fantastic," Macy says, and there's a hint of something more in her voice.

I seize the chance. "Want another? We can go to Doctor Insomnia's and—"

"Have a piece of cake instead?"

"Cake is definitely a good idea. Is cake one of your ways of making me talk?"

She smiles at me, a coquettish look in her eyes, like we have a secret. "I suppose we'll see."

"I think I'll like this way. I think I'll like it very much."

* * *

We order two teas and a slice of chocolate cake to share, and as Tommy hands the plate to me, he gives me a sly nod. "Go for it," he hisses as Macy walks to the table.

"All in due time," I hiss back. I return for the mugs then join Macy in the corner of the shop. We trade bites of cake, along with praise for this dessert. Midway through, she sets down her fork. "Why do you hate Valentine's Day?"

I exhale and tell her the truth. "I was cursed when I was eleven."

She laughs, but when I don't laugh back, she schools her expression.

But then I chuckle too. "Look, it's silly, but I was truly cursed."

"You really believe that?"

"Yes, no, maybe?"

I give her the details—the broken nose, Lily Van Tassel, and the hex that started it all.

"Fine. So you had a spate of bad luck. I get that. I had the opposite—lots of good luck on this day."

I sneer, not liking this direction. "With men?"

She scoffs then laughs as she pats my hand. "Don't be silly. I meant good luck in life. And listen, I don't think you were hexed, and I also don't think you need to love Valentine's Day, but I hope you'll realize it's truly just a day to celebrate friendship and love. You should embrace it a little bit."

Friendship. There's that word again. Is that all she wants? Or does she want the latter?

"Even if I get another broken nose?"

She glances around. "Who's going to break your nose? Tommy?"

"Let's hope not."

She studies my nose as she curls her hands around her mug of tea. Softly, she says, "I like your crooked nose."

"You do?"

She nods, swallowing. "I like your whole face."

My body hums with excitement, with the thrill of a compliment from the woman I adore. "I like yours too." Holy shit. Did that just happen? Did I just compliment her in a way that makes it patently obvious how I feel? Maybe I did, and maybe it works. The woman is smiling like she has a secret.

"How should I embrace it?"

"Well, you did get me a heart-covered latte earlier. I'd say that's a start."

But yet, I know there are other ways I should embrace the day. By talking to her, getting to know her even better, understanding her. "Tell me why you love it."

A brightness seems to stretch across her whole being. "I love friends and family and celebration. I've loved telling people I care about that I love them. That's what I think birthdays and holidays are all about. Showing people you love that you care."

The way she says that touches into the dark, jaded, cursed part of my heart and makes it lighter. "You're good at that."

"When I was younger, I made cards for everyone. Friends, family. I would tell them all the things I loved about them."

"That's a cool thing to do."

She shrugs like this is all second nature to her, and I suppose it is. "If you care about someone, you should let them know. I know you might think I love holidays because I'm a cornball and a former cheerleader and generally an extrovert."

I smile. "You are definitely an extrovert."

"And you're an introvert."

"I am?"

"You spend your evenings reading books."

"Hey, I work out too and go to sporting events."

"But that's the only thing you get excited about. The rest you keep inside."

"What do you think I'm keeping inside?"

"It's not what I think you're keeping inside. It's what I hope."

I'm warm everywhere, buzzing and hoping and wanting. "What do you hope for?"

But before she can answer, my phone rings. It's my sister. "Are you still near the rehearsal space? I left my laptop there."

"I'll head over and check." I hang up.

Macy stands up. "I'll go with you."

"Yeah?"

She rolls her eyes. "Why is that a surprise?"

"I don't know. You always do nice things. It shouldn't be a surprise."

"I like spending time with you, Kirby."

My skin heats to August in New York levels. "I like spending time with you too. I like it a lot. And if this is part of you having ways, you can keep having your way."

She raises an eyebrow in appreciation.

It sure feels like we're speeding out of the friend zone. And maybe that's not the worst thing in the world.

7

Kirby

On the hunt for my sister's laptop, we head to the building where we record. We step into the elevator, shooting up to the sixth floor.

A red sign in the elevator reads *Happy Valentine's Day*. Yesterday, I might have scowled at it. Today, though, thanks to talking to Macy, I consider that maybe I'm wrong. What if I've been wrong about everything? What if I've been wrong about curses? Besides, tomorrow is Valentine's Day. Today is still just a day.

I hit the stop button. Take a chance. "You want to know how much I like spending time with you?"

Her eyes widen, and her breathing seems to quicken. "I do."

I reach for her hand and bring her close. "For a long time, I've thought Valentine's Day sucked. I've considered it a social construct. I'm not saying it's my favorite day, but you're making me rethink a lot of things. Including something I'd like right now."

"What's that?"

"To kiss you in an elevator." Her eyes sparkle and say yes. I pull her against me and I kiss her hard and breathlessly. So hard I wonder why we've waited this long, but of course, I know all the reasons why we've waited this long.

Because I've waited.

Because I've been afraid.

Because I've had so much bad luck, I didn't believe I could have good luck.

I cup her cheek and sweep my thumb over her jaw, trying to erase the bad luck. To make our own new luck. She shudders in my arms and we kiss feverishly, like we've both been waiting years for this.

She moves closer, loops her arms around my neck, and threads her fingers in my hair. I kiss her more deeply —she's so damn soft and she tastes so damn sweet, and all I want is to take her home and have her and tell her. Tell her I'm not such a curmudgeon, I'm not such a grump. That if I could have her forever, she'd feel like the best luck.

She breaks the kiss and looks up at me, hazy-eyed. "I've been hoping you would do that."

"Is that so?"

"I've been wanting it for a long, long time."

Go for it. Go all the way in. Don't hold back. "Then I think we should do it for longer, like maybe all night."

Her grin is my yes, then she gives it to me in words. "I'd like that too."

I hit the button so we resume the pace, get off at the sixth floor, grab the laptop, and return to the elevator.

Once inside, I grab her face and kiss her again, softer this time, slow and lingering, savoring her. When the elevator arrives at the lobby and the doors open, my sister is waiting on the other side.

8

Kirby

I don't embarrass easily.

But here in the building, with my sister staring slack-jawed at me, I'm pretty sure my face is approximating a tomato.

It's probably not my best look, and I'm also certain I'm in big trouble. "Ally, sorry. Let me explain."

She holds up her hands, shaking her head. "There's nothing to explain."

I grab Ally's shoulder. Worry cartwheels through me. "But let me try."

"There's no need. I couldn't be happier you two were making out."

"For real?" I scratch my jaw, processing this new intel.

"For real. Now gimme my laptop and go forth and fornicate."

Macy laughs, shaking her head. "Gee, thanks, Ally."

"Admit it. It's a good idea," Ally adds.

I couldn't agree more. "Have I mentioned you're the best sister ever?"

She waves, backing up. "Go for it—finally."

Then she's gone, and I turn to Macy and do precisely that. I do what I should have done every single day since I met her. "Hey, you and I should be a thing."

She smiles like I've given her the keys to the world. "Are you saying you kind of want me to be your valentine?"

I groan, but it's a playful one. I tug her close, plant a kiss on her lips, and whisper, "Be mine."

Softly, she answers me. "I'm yours." She takes a beat and murmurs, "But I want you to know why I love Valentine's Day."

"For the hearts and stuff?" I ask carefully, since I might not be a Vrooge, but I'm not ready to don a Valentine's Day ugly sweater. Do they even make those? I bet they do.

But Macy doesn't seem to be thinking of ugly sweaters. A naughty glint crosses her eyes. "Yes, and for many other things. I also like it for the spicy side." Her tone is so damn sultry and inviting.

I slide a hand around her waist. "Is that so?"

Ever so innocently, she smiles, then seems to confess, "I have a bit of a naughty side."

I curl my fingers tighter around her. And my luck is officially changed. "I want to get to know that side."

"You didn't think I had a naughty side?"

"I had no idea."

"Why do you think I mentioned cinnamon?"

"Was I supposed to understand something about a cinnamon comment?"

"Cinnamon is spicy. It's not sweet."

I groan. "Are you telling me you're spicy instead of sweet?"

She dots a kiss to my nose. "I'm telling you I'm both. Do you want both tonight?"

9

Kirby

On the streets of New York, she tugs her shirt down her shoulder and shows me the red strap of her bra. I'm a goner.

Lust cascades in my body. As soon as my brain works again, I call an Uber and get her to my place ASAP.

In my building, we step into the lift and don't even bother to wait. "There's just something about elevators," I say as I kiss her again.

"They're not sweet and innocent. They're naughty and dirty."

"Are you naughty and dirty, Macy?"

"I want to be with you."

Holy shit. This is too much. This is a dream. A crazy, fevered dream because Macy wants the same things I do.

Macy's eyes light up. "Would you want to be like that with me?"

Lust sizzles through my body and I rasp out, "Yes."

We make it to my apartment, and before the door slams shut, I kiss her harder and more passionately than before. My hands find their way up her shirt, where I cup the red satin of her bra.

I lift her shirt and tug it off, and holy cupid. "You're so fucking sexy."

She nibbles on her lip. "I bought it for you. I wore it for you. It's all for you."

I slide a hand between her legs, cupping her through her jeans. I can feel the heat. I undo the zipper and slide my hand inside.

"That's why I like Valentine's Day." She trembles as I touch her where she wants. "Because it's sexy. Because it's hot. Because I don't just like you." She stares at me with lust in her irises. "I want you to fuck me, Kirby. I want you to fuck me today and tomorrow and the next day. I want you to do all sorts of crazy things to me."

Hallelujah. This is absolutely the best day ever.

I admire the red lingerie. "I no longer hate red," I say.

"I'm glad because I have all sorts of pretty lingerie. Red, pink, white, all those colors you think you don't like."

"Oh, I love them now," I tell her as her hands dart out to tug at my shirt and pull it over my head, and then to unfasten the zipper on my jeans.

I strip off her jeans and push her against the door. "So you like it spicy," I say in her ear. "Want me to fuck you up against the wall?"

"Please, yes."

I find a condom from my wallet as she shoves down my boxer briefs and grabs my cock. I shudder as she grips me, her fist sliding up and down my flesh. I roll the protection on, hitch up her leg, and slide inside.

It's incredible. It's intoxicating. It's mind-bending as pleasure rolls through me at the feel of being inside this woman—*the* woman I've been lusting after, liking, crushing on, wanting for the last few years.

As I take her against the door, she wraps her arms around my neck, tugging me as close as possible, whispering in my ear, "I love it like this. I want it like this. Do it harder."

And I do, listening to her every request and fulfilling them as I go deeper and she starts to lose control, shaking and shuddering, murmuring in my ear, groaning my name, and then soon enough, she's coming on my cock.

Pleasure spirals in me, coils tighter, until I follow her to the other side of pleasure.

* * *

After a glass of wine, Macy's ready for another round.

I back her up against the kitchen counter. "I bet you're wet and hot again," I whisper.

She trembles. "Find out."

I dip my hand between her legs, feeling her slick heat. "Look at you. So hot for the bad luck guy."

"It's not bad luck anymore."

I glide my fingers across her core, and she shudders, pushing against me. "Does the sweet dirty girl want to be fucked with my fingers?"

"I do," she says on a pant.

She's so fucking wet, so slippery against my hand as I slide a finger inside, then another. She grinds down, and I push deeper, hooking my fingers just so.

"Oh God," she says.

The way she lets go, the way she owns her pleasure,

is the most erotic thing. I'm no longer finger-fucking her. She's fucking my hand. She's grinding down on me, her breath uneven, her lids squeezed shut, her lips parted, as she shamelessly chases her pleasure.

"Fuck, Macy. You're so sexy."

"More. Give me more."

I slide my finger toward her ass, and she groans wildly. I press against her, and she cries out. "You like that, dirty girl?"

She nods savagely. She can't form words.

But she doesn't need to. Her body makes her wishes clear. My sweet Macy likes ass play. And I'd like to play with her ass. With two fingers in her pussy, I push one more against her ass.

A little more.

A little farther.

She yelps, but it turns into a carnal, guttural moan as I slide my finger into her. And she goes wild, fucking and humping and coming like a goddamn rock star.

When she comes down from her high, I ease out of her, step to the sink, and wash my hands. Picking her up, I toss her over my shoulder and carry her to my bedroom.

I lower her to the bed where she smiles woozily at me as I press a kiss to her belly button. Then her hip. Then the top of her mound.

"Oh God, are you going to do more to me?"

"If you want me to."

She reaches for my face. "I want you to go down on me, but I want something else first."

"Name it," I say, thinking I hit the fucking jackpot with this woman. Friendship, feelings, and a big bedroom appetite.

"Can I suck your cock first?"

Like I'm saying no to that. "Fuck yeah." My dick throbs, a drop of liquid forming at the tip just from her question.

"But there's something I want you to do."

"What's that?"

"Don't be gentle."

Lust seizes every cell of my body. "Jesus, woman. You are fiery."

"Too fiery?"

"There's no such thing."

"Then I want something else too."

"Anything."

She smiles coyly, slides to the floor, and gets down on her knees. She links her hands behind her back, restraining her own wrists. "Fuck my mouth."

And I'm on fire. Hot, dirty desire rattles through my bones as I do as asked, controlling the best blow job of my life, fucking her mouth, filling her, racing to the edge.

When I reach it, I see stars. They flicker behind my eyes as pleasure speeds white-hot through me as I release in her throat.

* * *

Later, she's curled up next to me, and I stroke her hair. "I had no idea you were so wild."

"Because you were afraid."

I nod, accepting that assessment. "I'm not afraid anymore. That's because of you." I cup her chin. "Because you were bold. Because you took a chance on me. Because you looked past my . . . *Vrooge-ness.*"

She cuddles against me. "I knew there was more to you. I've always seen it. I just wanted you to move a little outside your comfort zone."

I run a hand along her flesh. "I like all these zones with you."

Worry crosses her eyes. "Do you only like me because I want it rough and dirty?"

I shake my head, laughing. "No, sweetheart. I like the sex, but it's always been you. The fact that you tell me what you want makes you even sexier. Because you ask for it."

She sighs happily, her fingers trailing along the ink on my arms. "I want to keep asking for it."

I pull her close. "I want you to keep asking for it. I want to keep giving it to you. And I want to give you more than sex, Macy. You know that, right?"

She nods, a wicked grin on her face. A grin of happiness. "I do know that, but I like hearing it."

"We can be friends and lovers. We can be everything." Suddenly, it's not hard to say how I feel. It's the easiest thing in the world, because she's given me confidence. She's changed all my luck.

"I want that."

"Good, because you're mine."

"I like being yours."

I glance at the clock. It's past midnight. It's the day I used to hate. But this woman brought me around, with her enthusiasm and her huge heart that I'm falling madly in love with. "Hey, Macy. Will you be my valentine?"

"Always."

10

From the texts of Ally & Miller

Ally: You will never believe what happened.

Miller: Tell me.

Ally: My brother. And Macy. In the elevator.

Miller: Were they doing the Macarena? The hula? Wait, a luau.

Ally: Stop. They were all over each other.

Miller: This is getting good. But define "all over."

Ally: Please. You know what I mean.

Miller: Yeah, but spell it out because it's more entertaining that way.

Ally: You want me to entertain you now with stories?

Miller: Don't I always want you to entertain me with stories?

Ally: You want me to entertain you with stories of what my brother was doing in the elevator?

Miller: When you put it like that, it's a little weird. And yet I still kind of want to hear it. But the question is, does this bother you?

Ally: Do you think it would bother me?

Miller: I don't know, aren't you pissed?

Miller: You want me to talk to him? Do you want me to come talk you down?

Miller: So you don't toss a trash can? Or go full Godzilla. Stomping like crazy through the city. I can see it now. You'd be all over the news.

Ally: Wow. Quite a scenario you paint.

Miller: Woman turns Godzilla when she sees her brother kissing her best friend.

Ally: You're insane. How does your mind even go there?

Miller: My mind's very active. I can picture all sorts of things.

Ally: Let me put it this way. They're not going to play Candy Land tonight.

Miller: I've heard about different versions of Candy Land.

Ally: And he goes to dirty joke land again.

Miller: No joking. So many versions now. I don't think Candy Land is the same as it used to be when we were kids.

Ally: I don't want to hear about how you played Candy Land.

Miller: Did I say I played it that way?

Ally: You're infuriating to talk to.

Miller: But you love talking to me.

Ally: Of course I do. So let me tell you what happened.

Miller: Wait. Just answer. Are you mad at them?

Ally: Are you seriously asking me?

Miller: Yes, of course, I'm asking you.

Miller: Are you mad at them?

Ally: No. I'm happy for them.

* * *

Miller: Note to self—remember that. She's happy for two friends who became lovers.

Miller: New note to self—but don't fool yourself into thinking it could work for the two of you.

Miller: New new note to self—no matter how much you want to change her mind.

11

Macy
  A month later

I catch a glimpse of a lacy white teddy in the lingerie shop. "Now that is what I want to wear for our one-month anniversary."

Olivia laughs. "Are you celebrating one month?"

I give her a *duh* look. "Of course. This is me. I love all kinds of celebrations. And Kirby does now too."

"Or does he just like you in white lace?"

I wink. "He loves me in white lace. And he also loves me."

"I knew he did. I knew he would. You were determined, and you went for it."

I bring the white teddy to the register. "And I'm going to keep going for it."

EPILOGUE

Kirby

Four years later

I sweep into the house, carrying a bouquet of roses, a box of candy, and a velvet box with a necklace. I find my wife in the kitchen, pouring champagne for me and seltzer water for her.

I kiss her cheek, her hair, and her lovely lips. "Hey, beautiful."

"Hey, you."

I run a hand over her swollen belly. "How do you feel?"

"Ready. Also, I got you a gift."

She hands me a box from a lingerie store. It's a red teddy. "I'll wear it again soon."

"Wear it when you're ready. Don't rush. I'll always be here."

"But lingerie was how I seduced you."

"Sweetheart, I think you're remembering it wrong. If

memory serves, I did kiss you senseless in an elevator the night before Valentine's Day."

Her eyes widen with surprise. "Huh. That's true. But I was so ready to seduce you with my red lingerie and everything. It felt like *I* went for it."

"You did. You kept talking to me. You got me to open up, and once I did, I made a move. We both made the right moves."

"We both went for it," she agrees.

I kiss her again, softly, gently, since sometimes she likes it that way. "And now that we've seduced each other, I should let you know you're stuck with me," I say, curling my palm over her stomach.

She runs a hand down my inked arm. My tattoos now include her name, just as Pete from the lobby predicted.

We might be a little dirty, a little naughty. We do like to experiment. We try different positions, different places, and sometimes I tie her up. I spank her and pull her hair. Sometimes she begs me for it.

She likes to beg for it.

And hell, do I love it when she does.

But then again, I love everything with my wife, and all our luck changed thanks to red lingerie, her, and a heart-shaped latte.

Or really, when I got my head out of my ass.

That helped too.

Let that be a lesson to other men. Be open to falling in love, because you might get so much more.

Love, friendship, and the woman you want to roll around with in the sheets.

"I'm definitely keeping you," she says, then her eyes widen and she clutches her belly. "It's time."

* * *

"Push! Push! You can do it."

And she does. My wife pushes out a beautiful baby girl and I fall in love with Macy all over again.

Our daughter is born on Valentine's Day.

It's fitting. Since that was the beginning of not just our love affair, but how I fell for the woman who fucked all the Vrooge out of me.

ANOTHER EPILOGUE

Ally

Well, it sure seems like everything worked out for Macy and Kirby. Love, friendship, and lots of nookie, or so I presume.

They're ridiculously happy and loving life together. They're still the best of friends and I'm friends with both of them too. But just because it worked for them doesn't mean it'll work for me with Miller.

Just because something works for someone else doesn't mean it'll work for you. So I remain cautious with Miller. I remain on this side of the fence.

Until my brother tells me that he's moving out of town with his wife and his daughter, and that's the beginning of everything starting to change with Miller and me.

THE END

Intrigued by Miller and Ally? They have a story to tell in the USA Today and Wall Street Journal Bestseller ONCE UPON A SURE THING, available everywhere.

TOO GOOD TO BE TRUE

ABOUT

To say I'm wary of love would be an epic understatement. Keep that four-letter word far away from me.

But then a matchmaker friend insists she can pair me with the perfect man for me.

Even when sparks fly and chemistry crackles from the first date, I refuse to believe this kind of insta-connection can be the real thing.

Even though for the first time it feels like it could be.

Or is it just too good to be true?

1

Olivia

Do I want to try it?

My brother asked me that very question when he invited me to check out a prototype for his new home automation system.

This is no Alexa. This is no Google Home. His home automation system supposedly answers your most annoying emails, makes you an omelet, and even folds your laundry.

Well, in my dream life it does.

Geek that I am, naturally I said "hell to the yes" when he invited me to take a test run. So here I am, race-walking across the blond hardwood floor of the lobby of his swank Gramercy Park building and pushing the button to his penthouse apartment.

When I reach the top floor, I practically vault down the hall to his place.

Can you say eager?

I bang on his door. He takes more than ten seconds to answer, so I decide to act thoroughly annoyed when he finally does.

"Come on, come on, come on." I'm bouncing on my toes, making grabby hands.

He rolls his eyes from behind his black glasses. "Overeager much?"

He holds the door open for me. I sweep in, my eyes like lasers scanning for the little white device. "You can't dangle something as cool as the ultimate home automation in front of me and expect me not to jump all over it and want to play with it. I only strapped a jetpack on and flew down to touch it."

He laughs, escorting me to the living room. He knows that, just like him, I love all sorts of electronics, gadgets, gizmos, and toys, and have ever since we were kids, fighting over all sorts of various game consoles. Since I'm the oldest, with two twin brothers, I usually beat them.

And I beat them up.

Someone had to put the little evil geniuses in their place. Lately, it's hard to put Dylan in his place since he's been traveling for business. But when he returns, I fully intend to kick his butt in our softball league.

"True, true," Flynn says thoughtfully. "What was I thinking? You and Dylan are both geeks like me."

I hold up a fist for knocking. "Dude, we are so nerdy. Also, FYI: nerds rule."

He scoffs authoritatively. "You know it. Nerd or bust."

I spy the device on the coffee table. My eyes widen and I hold out my hands, like I'm caught in a tractor beam. "Take me to your leader."

"Kate is all yours," he says, using the name of the automation device.

I park myself in the leather couch and fire off questions.

"Kate, tell me a dog joke."

"Kate, make me a sandwich."

"Kate, what's the weather like in Bora Bora?"

She answers each one with panache.

What's more amazing than a talking dog? A spelling bee.

Okay, you're a sandwich.

And . . .

Perfect, you should go there.

I glance at Flynn, who's rightfully proud of his new tech. "Kate knows the answers to everything. I'm booking a flight now."

Flynn nods his agreement. "Bora Bora is always a good idea. If anyone thinks otherwise, you should excise him or her from your life."

I tap my temple. "The Bora Bora litmus test. I'm filing that away." I return my focus to the white disc. "Kate, make me a playlist of top pop songs."

As she preps some Ariana Grande and Katy Perry, Flynn groans and drops his head into his hand.

"No, please, no pop songs."

"I like pop."

"You need to try indie rock, I've told you."

I roll my eyes and launch into my best rendition of his favorite tunes. "Oh, my life is so sad, I flew with an eagle, and now I have a noose around my toes."

He cracks up and gives me the strangest look. "What on earth is that, Olivia?"

I answer like it's obvious. "That's what indie sounds like. A sad lament."

"Oh, well then, let me tell you what pop sounds like."

Flynn adopts an intensely happy look, snapping his fingers, then sings a send-up of my music. "Oh, I want you. Yes I do. Yes, yes, yes, I do. Do do do do do do do do do."

I laugh. "See, that's so fun to listen to! You should totally write that song."

"So we agree to disagree on music."

"But not the Bora Bora litmus test."

"Never the Bora Bora litmus test."

I spend the next hour playing with the device, and pronounce it is the coolest one I've ever seen. "But we have one more test for Kate."

"What is it?"

I hold my arms out wide, like I'm ready to make a pronouncement. "This will be the toughest test of all. Can she handle what I'm going to throw at her?"

Flynn gestures grandly. "Go for it."

I clear my throat, adopting a most serious tone. "Kate, find me a hot, smart, and kind guy. Must love animals. Be willing to try quirky new dates in New York City. Ideally, likes odd and interesting art installations. And be able to sustain a conversation about something other than himself."

Flynn's eyes bulge. "She's not a miracle worker," he says protectively. He's protective of the device.

Kate speaks back in her calming robotic voice, but I've rattled her. "I'm sorry, that does not compute. Can you please try again?"

I crack up.

"You can't really expect her to do the impossible," Flynn says.

"I know, tell me about it."

He leans forward, hands on his knees. "So is dating getting you down?"

I sigh. "A little bit. It's kind of awful out there. Have you tried it lately?"

He shudders. "No, I'm practically on a sabbatical since Annie."

I shudder too, remembering Flynn's ex. She turned out to be completely using him, trying to sink her claws into his fortune. Not for nothing, but it's really hard for a tech multimillionaire to find somebody who likes him for him. My brother is rich as sin, and normally I don't feel bad for him, but on this count—never knowing if someone loves you for you or your money—my heart is heavy.

It's a poor little rich boy dilemma, as he calls it. Yet it's wholly real.

"But what about you? What's the latest from the minefield of dating?"

"Last night I went out with a handsome surgeon, who was all around pretty funny and smart. But it turns out he's into jazz music," I say, crinkling my nose. "He spent half the time telling me he loves to go to jazz clubs *and* to listen to jazz at home. I had to be honest—jazz is never going to be part of my life, so we're clearly not compatible. We'd never see each other."

Flynn gives me a look, takes a deep breath. "Olivia. But are you doing it again?"

"Doing what?" I ask, indignant. "Being direct and honest on dates about what works and doesn't work?"

"Are you sabotaging every date you go on?"

I sit up straight. "I do not do that."

He points at me. "Yes, you do."

"I don't care for jazz."

"I'm sure you could have found a work-around for his love of jazz. Instead, you sabotage. You've done that ever since Ron."

I huff. "Do you blame me? Ron was the ultimate douchenozzle. And he hid it well."

"'Douchenozzle' is a bit tame for that specimen. More like 'king of all the assholes ever.' It's not often you find a man who's not only a cheater but a serial cheater. He had affairs like it was an advent calendar."

A twinge of embarrassment stings my chest. "And that makes me the stupidest woman ever for missing the signs?"

Flynn moves next to me, squeezing my shoulder. "No. You liked the guy, and he was the Artful Dodger. It was hard to spot his deception at first. But ever since then, when you've met a guy here or there who seems somewhat decent, you always find something wrong with him. A smart and funny surgeon? But he likes jazz, so that's a deal-breaker? And then you tell him?"

"But I don't like jazz one bit," I say in a small voice.

"Look, I don't like jazz either. But I don't think it needs to be a line in the sand." He arches a brow. "Be honest with me. Are you constantly looking for what's wrong with a man so you won't get hurt again?"

I sigh, wishing it wasn't so obvious, but then Flynn knows me as well as anyone. "I was totally hoodwinked by Ron. I didn't see it coming, and I should have. What if it happens again?" I ask, my deepest worry coloring my tone.

"Anything can happen, but now you try to find something wrong with someone before you even start. You're never going to open yourself to what you want if you do that."

I cross my arms, exhale heavily. "Fine, maybe I do that, but look, I haven't met anybody that ticks all the boxes on my checklist. Or even three quarters. Hell, I'd settle for half. I don't even know if my dream guy exists."

He stares out the window, like he's considering a math problem. Since my brother solves math problems in his sleep, he snaps his fingers. "My buddy Patrick. His sister is a matchmaker."

"A real matchmaker? Like Yente?" I sing a few lines from *Fiddler on the Roof*.

"Of course, you have to sing that every time you see her. It's literally required. Why don't you try Evie? Let her know what you're looking for. Maybe she can find someone for you."

I've tried online dating. I've been set up by friends. I've been open to meeting men at the gym, at bookstores, even at the farmers market. But I've had no luck finding a jazz hater, animal lover, quirky-art fan, who's hot as hell and likes me.

"Admittedly, I'm kind of picky. Do you think I'm better off being single?"

"Olivia, you want to be happy. You want to find someone. Just call Evie. Her job is to find matches for picky people."

That sounds exactly like me.

And because I'm not boneheaded, I do call her. I meet with her the next day at a coffee shop.

She's everything you want in a matchmaker. She has a keen eye for people; she's perky, wildly outgoing, fantastically upbeat; and she knows everyone.

"Are my requirements just too crazy?" I ask after I've told her what I'm looking for.

Evie gives me a reassuring look and pats my hand. "No. You don't have requirements that are too hard to meet. What's too hard is to find a man like that online. But that's why you came to me." Her smile is radiant and full of confidence. "I have a few men in mind. Just give me a couple of days, and I promise I will do everything I can to find you the man of your dreams."

It sounds impossible to me.

2

Herb

"Hey there, little Cletus. You're doing great, and you look swell," I tell the teacup chihuahua with the burnished brown coat. He whimpers as I stroke a hand down his soft back. Cletus is resting in a cage after the five-month-old had a very important surgery today. "Don't worry," I whisper. "You won't miss them."

My vet tech snickers behind me. "Bet he will."

I roll my eyes at David as I turn around. "I see you're suffering from neutering sympathy. Shall I get him a pair of neuticles to make you feel better?"

"That would help me a lot, come to think of it."

"You do know he doesn't miss them?"

David grabs his crotch. "I'd miss mine."

"Then it's a good thing I'm not neutering you, isn't it?"

At twenty-three, David is still young, and his age

might be why he still feels that associative pain that men often experience when a dog is neutered. At age thirty-four, and after thousands of spays and neuters, I'm well beyond that. I don't get emotional over removing that particular part of a dog's anatomy. And I don't get weirded out.

It's all in a day's work.

David gives me a salute. "Yes, boss. Also, Cletus's foster mom is here."

"Great. I'll go chat with Evie." She's a regular foster for one of the city's nearby rescues, bringing in little dogs for their nip and tucks as they're getting ready to be adopted.

Gently, I scoop up the pup and carry the coneheaded boy to the lobby of my practice on the Upper East Side.

Evie waves brightly at me. "And how is the sweet little boy?"

"He did great."

Evie laughs. "Now, I always thought it was kind of funny to say that an animal did great during a surgery. Because, really, isn't it *you* who did great during a surgery?" She taps my shoulder affectionately.

She has a point.

And I concede to it, blowing on my fingernails for effect. "When you've got it, you've got it. No one snips dog balls better than this guy."

"Put that on your business card, Herb."

"It'll be my new tagline." I shift gears. "All right, you know the drill. Give him plenty of rest, make sure he takes it easy. He might not want to eat right away. And whatever you do, keep that lampshade on him."

Evie drops her face into the dog's tiny cone and gives him a kiss. "I won't let you get out of your cone, I promise, Coney Boy."

"Give me a call if anything comes up, okay? Day or night. Doesn't matter."

"That sounds perfect." But before she turns to leave, she gives me a look. It's a look that says she has something on her mind. "Dr. Smith, I've been meaning to ask you something."

"I can see the wheels turning in your head."

She smiles, acknowledging that I'm right. "Have you started dating again? It's been more than a year or so since Sandy left."

"Yes, I've dated," I say, a little defensively. "I just haven't met the right person."

"It's hard to meet the right person. I hear you on that front." Her tone is sympathetic.

"I thought I *had* met the right person."

The thing is Sandy was a fantastic woman, and I can't fault her for leaving. She was offered a fantastic job in Beijing. She accepted and boarded a flight two weeks later without any fanfare or discussions about us continuing.

We'd been together for a year. We'd started making plans. And then her plan was to move halfway around the world, so that's what she did, ending us in one clean slice.

"But you can't let it get you down," Evie adds. "You are a prize."

I straighten my shoulders and flash an over-the-top smile. "Thank you. I always thought I'd look really nice paraded around onstage, perhaps given away at the end of a blue ribbon ceremony."

"We'll enter you in a dating contest." She sighs thoughtfully, her eyes narrowing a bit as she taps her chin with her free hand. "But I have other ideas for you."

"Fess up. Are you trying to enlist me into your stable again?"

She swats my arm affectionately. "Of course. I've only been trying to get you in my stable for ages. You know that. Smart, single, sweet as anything, clever, hot vet who does free spay and neuter clinics for the city's rescues? You are going to be in demand."

Since she's a premiere matchmaker, Evie's broached the subject before. I've been reluctant though. Maybe I've been nursing my wounds since my ex took off with barely a goodbye kiss. Or maybe a part of me figures if I can put myself through vet school, open a successful practice, and make it in Manhattan, I ought to be able to find a woman without a little assistance. "Honestly, I figured I'd meet someone the old-fashioned way, like how I met Sandy. We bumped into each other at a coffee shop. She nearly spilled her hot chocolate on me."

"Ah, the old rom-com meet-cute."

"Well, yeah. I suppose it was. So I assumed I'd meet someone new in a similar fashion."

"And how's that working out for you?"

I scratch my jaw, considering her question. "Badly."

"You don't say?"

"Do I detect a note of mockery?"

"No. I simply agree that it's as hard as differential calculus to hope to meet someone in person in a random, swoony, just-like-the-movies way."

"I've been on dates. Mostly setups from friends."

"And?"

I wince, shaking my head. "Dreadful. I'd rather bathe in molasses than go out with another *oh, Tonya knows so-and-so and so-and-so knows so-and-so*. And what it truly amounts to is this—your one single friend was pressured by his girlfriend or fiancée to set up her one single friend, and it doesn't matter if you have anything in common."

She nods sympathetically as she strokes Cletus's head. "That is indeed the problem with friends setting up friends simply by virtue of their relationship status. I, however, have a long list of lovely single ladies, and I only connect people I think—no, I'm sure—will go together like gin and tonic."

"I do like a good gin and tonic."

She smiles impishly. "I know. All my clients are vetted and interested in the real deal. And I know you're interested in that too."

"How do you know?" I'm curious why she says that, but truth be told, she nailed it on the head.

"That's what you wanted with Sandy. You're not somebody who goes out and plays the field, Herb."

She's right on that count. "That's true."

She stares at me, determination etched in her blue eyes. "So, what's it going to be, Mister Meow?"

I groan. "No. That nickname is unacceptable."

"I promise I won't call you that again if you'll let me match you."

"So it's coercion now, eh?" The woman is relentless with her cheer and optimism.

"Call it coercion, or call it kismet. Whatever you call it, I have the perfect woman for you."

I raise a skeptical brow. "What if she's boring?"

She shakes her head. "Not a chance."

I toss out another concern. "What if she's shallow?"

"She's bright and thoughtful."

And one more hurdle. "What if she, I dunno, smells?"

Evie leans in closer and taps my nose with her finger. "She smells pretty, you silly man."

Then the deal-breaker. "What if she doesn't like dogs?"

"Give me some credit. As if I'd set you up with someone who doesn't like dogs. The woman I have in mind is lovely. She's been looking to adopt just the right three-legged dog."

And my heart melts a little bit. Wait, wait. I can't. I can't fall for her that quickly, I don't even know her. "I suppose one date can't hurt. But I don't want to do dinner."

"Dinner is off the table."

"I don't want to do a wine tasting."

"Just say no to the vino."

"I don't want to do a beer tasting, and I don't want to do something that's like super hipster-y, like a mayonnaise tasting or pickle tasting."

"Got it. You probably don't want to do a carrot tasting either, then. Do you?"

"Do people really have carrot tastings?"

"Have you been to Brooklyn? They have everything these days."

"True that."

"You want to do something totally unconventional. Something that will let you know if you have chemistry."

That's the thing. I've done the whole typical three dates thing a handful of times ever since Sandy left, and I don't want to get on that merry-go-round again. "I just want to get on the merry-go-round once for one date, and I'll know after one date."

"Then it needs to be one spectacular date. Do you still like bizarre, oddball, quirky modern art?"

"Damn, you have a good memory."

"I have a memory for matches. Would you like to meet a smart, sarcastic, tech-savvy art lover who likes to discover all the interesting things about New York and who loves puzzles?"

My ears perk up. "I love puzzles."

3

Olivia

"How do I look?" I ask my brother on the other side of the phone via video chat.

His green eyes light up with laughter and, admittedly, a whole ton of mockery. "How do you look?" he echoes.

I bristle. "I need a guy's opinion."

"And you asked me?" He points to his chest.

"I'm pretty sure you're a guy. Is there something you want to tell me? Did you swap your parts?"

"No, but my point is, I'm your brother. It basically disqualifies me from ever commenting on your appearance."

I huff. "Can you just tell me if I look good?"

"No, I actually can't tell you. I couldn't function any longer as a man in any way if I tell my sister she looks good. Fine, empirically, yes. You look good. But you also look stupid because you're my sister, and I have to think that."

"You legitimately cannot think your sister looks nice in something? I'm thirty, you're twenty-seven. We're not children anymore."

"Doesn't matter. Certain things can never change. You look fine. Sisters always look fine. I can't give you any other opinion than that."

I stare daggers at him. "Flynn, it's a good thing I like you. And you know what? I like myself too, so I am going to assume that I chose wisely in the fashion department."

He flashes a smile. "There you go. That's the confident sis I know and love. You did choose wisely. Now go out and have a great time. I'm so psyched that you used Evie. I have a good feeling about this. Don't sabotage it."

"Who, me?" I ask ever so innocently. "I would never do that."

His expression goes stern. "I mean it, Liv."

I hold up my free hand in oath. "I promise. I installed an anti-sabotage shield on myself tonight. And I am going into this with eyes wide open."

We say goodbye, and I give myself a final once-over in the mirror.

Jeans look good, boots look sexy, cute top that slips off one shoulder is pretty, with a hint of something more. My brown hair sports a little wave as it curls over my shoulders.

"You are a thumbs-up," I tell my reflection.

I head downtown to Tribeca to meet Herb, the hot vet.

* * *

I arrive right on time, expecting him to be late. Most people usually are. But when I see a tall, trim, toned, handsome, as in the most handsome in the entire universe, man standing in front of a light installation at the Helen Williams Gallery, my breath catches.

There's no way that's him.

That guy in the dark jeans and a blue button-down shirt that hugs his muscles has to be somebody else. I bet he was flown in, shipped in from some foreign country that grows good-looking men in meadows. He was paid to stand around and simply radiate handsome. He has to be a model. There's no way that's actually Herb, the hot vet, standing under a fuchsia-pink light, exactly where Evie said to look for him.

Herb is probably in the restroom and this stepped-out-of-a-magazine-ad man is holding his spot.

But then Mr. Too Handsome for Words catches my gaze. His lips quirk up in a lopsided smile that puts all the other lopsided smiles in the entire universe to shame. Because that is the crooked smile that defines why crooked smiles are absolutely delicious. Already my stomach is flipping, and I haven't even talked to him.

"What do you think? Is pink my color?" he asks from a few feet away, glancing up at the light.

God, I hope it's him. I walk closer. "I see you as more of a magenta."

He gives me a thoughtful look. "That's too bad. I was actually hoping perhaps I would be a periwinkle."

I laugh. "Do you know what periwinkle looks like?"

"No, isn't it a shade of, let me guess, blue?" He extends a hand. "I'm Herb Smith."

Praise the Lord. "I'm Olivia Parker."

Herb Smith is the most handsome man I've ever met, with his dark hair, square jaw, and blue eyes the sapphire color of perfect Bora Bora ocean. The man is to die for, and I don't believe in playing games. If I'm going to be up-front with the duds, I'll be direct with the un-duds.

"I didn't think the man standing under the light was actually going to be you," I admit, going for full truth.

"Why's that?"

I gulp, and then I bite off a big chunk of honesty, since what's the point in anything else? "You look like you were imported from the land of hot men."

He blinks. His eyes widen and sparkle, and then he says, "Wow. I didn't know that country existed."

"It's right between Goodlookingvia and Stunninglandenero. Just north of Beautifulcountria."

"I'd like to see your map of the world."

"I have it at home. But was that too forward? Calling you good-looking and objectifying you from the start? Want me to rewind and go again?"

"Hold on a second. You just complimented me for being too handsome, and you think that was too forward?"

"In case you think I'm only evaluating you based on your appearance," I say, since I had the impression from Evie that her services are more of the soul mate variety and less of the hop-on-the-hottie style.

He runs a hand lightly down my arm. "Judge me some more. I should be so lucky."

He drops his arm and I smile, the kind that stretches across my whole face. "In fact," he adds, "I hope you have a long list of traits you're going to be evaluating me on, like a checklist?"

I wave a hand dismissively. "I have that list on my smartphone. I'll fill it out tonight. After we see how this goes."

"How long is that list?"

I stare up at the ceiling, pretending I'm deep in thought. "I'd say it's about five or six pages."

"You're a woman after my own heart."

"Do you have a long checklist?"

"I do, and it's incredibly long." He takes a beat, his baby blues strolling up and down my body. "Lots of things are incredibly long."

"Who's forward now?" I ask, acting all aghast, but I'm not aghast at all. I like long things.

"What can I say? It seemed apropos. By the way, I'm not imported. I was actually locally grown."

"Ah, so you're a farm-to-date man?"

"Yes, I was homegrown within a fifty-mile radius. Raised in Westchester. So you're really able to tick a ton of boxes tonight. Presuming farm-to-date is on that *long* checklist."

"I'm adding it now and checking it off," I say, and inside I am punching the sky.

This is the best date ever.

As the pink glow from the neon light installation flickers behind him, I decide to opt for more honesty since it seems to be working so far—and way better than sabotage, it turns out. "I probably shouldn't say this, but dating can seriously suck, and in the first ten minutes, you're more fun than anyone I've gone out with in a long time, and on top of that, you're an insanely handsome guy." I park my hands on my hips, narrowing my eyes. "What's wrong with you?"

He heaves a sigh. "Fine. I'll admit it. I'm terrible at following IKEA directions for putting furniture together. I know, you just follow the steps. But it's hard, and I am bad at it. Can you live with that?"

I frown, scrub a hand across my chin. "If I have to."

He steps closer, his eyes taking a tour again. "Also,

you beat me to it. You're beautiful. But honestly, even if you were average looking, that would be fine too, because looks aren't the most important thing, and these first few minutes are my favorite too. In a long time."

Holy shit. He's a breath of rarified air. I'm smiling, he's grinning, his eyes are sparkling, and my insides are shimmy shimmy bang banging. "I agree. Looks aren't all that."

"So we're good, then? If you bore me, I'm gonna be out of here in like a half hour."

"That long? I'd have thought sooner. But I'm glad that the challenge is on, and it goes both ways. You better keep up with me, Herb Smith."

"Oh, I intend to. I absolutely intend to keep up with you."

We wander around the gallery, checking out the bizarre installations made of neon lights, and as we go, my skin warms, my heart squeezes, and my hope skyrockets. I like this guy, I like his ease of conversation. I like the way he snaps, crackles, and pops when he talks.

I bet there's something wrong with him though.

Except I can't go looking.

I need to maintain the anti-self-sabotage shield.

We stop in front of a bright yellow pair of neon lights that look like a balloon animal at certain angles. "Also, can we get one thing out of the way real quick?" he asks.

I slice a hand in the air. "There's not going to be any sex tonight."

Laughter seems to burst from him. "That's not what I was going to say, but it's good to know your ground rules. Just so we're clear, are all types of sex off the table?"

Twin spots of pink form on my cheeks. "Probably."

He steps closer, and I can smell him—his aftershave

is woodsy and intoxicating. "What about kissing, can we kiss? Let's say that I meet some of the marks on your checklist, do you want to have a kiss at the end?" he asks, and I'm nearly drunk on him already.

I want a kiss right the hell now. "That seems reasonable," I say a little breathy. Then my mind trips back to his comment. "What did you want to get out of the way, then?"

He takes a deep breath. "Yes, Herb is my real name."

"I didn't think it was a fake name."

"Who would pick that as a fake name, unless you were trying to scare somebody off?"

"Your name doesn't scare me," I say, because I'm 100 percent unperturbed by his old-school name.

"Are you sure?"

I point to the light sculpture on the white wall. "I'm still standing here under this weird, bizarre, twisty-turny collage of rainbow neon lights. I'm sure."

He glances up at the art installation in question. "Isn't that the coolest thing?"

"It's so weird, it's like the perfect weird piece of art. I want to hang that in my apartment and have people come over and say, 'What is that?' And I'll reply with 'my innermost thoughts,'" I say, all haughty.

"You're devilish," he says in admiration.

"Perhaps I am."

I stare at him, amazed that it's already going this well. "By the way, why did you mention your name?"

His tone is softer, more direct. "I guess because I'm surprised you didn't. Most dates bring up my name, since it's unusual. They want to know if it's a nickname, if it's real, if it's a family name that my mom *had* to give me. Or a mistake."

"A mistake? Why would someone think it's a mistake?"

He shoots me a steely glare. "Herb? Let's cut to the chase. It ain't Chase. It isn't Hunter or Bennett or Foxface, or whatever cool names dudes have these days."

A smile crosses my lips, warming me from the inside out. "I don't give a foxface if your name is cool or uncool. But is there a story behind it?"

He chuckles in a self-deprecating way that's thoroughly endearing. "Herb was my granddad's name. It was supposed to be my middle name. But he passed away a few days before I was born, and well, my sentimental parents made it my first name."

"Aww. That's touching. A very sweet story."

"I'm stuck with it, but he was a great man, so it's all good. And I have the world's simplest last name, so go figure."

"I like both of your names. The juxtaposition of the old-fashioned next to the familiar is a refreshing combo. It makes you even more unique, like this date."

"Normally on dates I count the seconds until it's going to be over."

"Ouch. The seconds, really? Is it usually that bad that you have to count the actual seconds?"

He nods vigorously. "It's usually that bad."

"What's the shortest date you've ever been on?" I query as we stroll through another hall of the art gallery.

"I would say about twelve minutes and fifty-two seconds. We had nothing to say to each other, and it was evident when she wanted to talk about how to do her nails, then she showed me an Instagram video of how to do nails, and there was like sponges and glue, and it was Instagram. Have I mentioned it was Instagram?"

"I'm going to go out on a limb and admit it. I do not

get the fascination with every single life hack for every single thing, for every type of makeup or every type of possible decoration you could put on your body or face, but it seems like everyone in a certain age range wants to do everything they've learned from Instagram."

He smiles. "Is it too early to say this is the best date I've been on in a long time?"

My grin matches his. "I don't think it's too early at all, but I think we really should reserve judgment until we finish the main attraction."

"Are you ready for it?"

"I'm so ready."

We finish the appetizer portion of our date and head over to devour the main course.

4

Herb

As we walk to the warehouse, we talk.

"Ever been to an escape room before?" We turn down a lively block in Tribeca.

She wiggles her eyebrows. "That sounds like a come-on."

"Maybe it is." I dive into an exaggerated seductive voice. "Want to come see my . . . escape room, baby?"

She purses her lips then drags a hand down her chest. "Oooh, yes. Show it to me now."

I growl, keeping up the routine, loving how easily I'm clicking with this woman. "Level with me. Are you an escape room virgin?"

She drops a demure expression on her face. "I am indeed."

"Me too," I say, returning to my normal voice. "But Evie thinks it's perfect for us since I love puzzles and you presumably do too."

"Crazy for them," she says, emphasizing the words with passion. "My job is kind of like a puzzle. Being an ethical hacker. You have to get into everything backward." Then she talks more about some of the work she does, and it's fascinating. She practices hacking into security for banks, then giving them advice on where they have holes. "And it's sort of similar to what you do," she says. "Which is a puzzle too."

Instantly I know what she means.

"Since my patients can't talk?"

She smiles and nods. "Yes, that does make it quite a puzzle. It's like you need a whole other language."

We chat more as we weave through the moonlit streets in lower Manhattan, and as we do, I take a moment to admire her. I was being honest when I said if she wasn't pretty, it wouldn't matter.

And I meant it. To me, this kind of chemistry—instant and electric—matters so much more.

But I still find it kind of hard to believe she's as gorgeous as she is, and as interesting as she is. Clearly, something has to go wrong, like it did with Sandy.

I tense momentarily, picturing my ex.

Seeing her face.

Feeling the gut punch of her news that she was leaving on a jet plane.

But I don't want Sandy to infect this night.

I hoist those thoughts right out of my mind.

We stop at a light, and I put a hand on Olivia's arm then run my palm down her skin. "I hope I'm not being too forward by touching your arm."

She gazes at me. "You can definitely touch my arm. In fact, I hope I'm not being too forward by saying it gave me the shivers."

"Good shivers?" I ask as a cab screams by.

"Definitely the good kind."

"I can work with good shivers."

The light changes and we cross. "Good shivers are another item on the checklist," she says.

I mime checking it off.

She flashes a smile that ignites me, and I wonder why I took so long to say yes to Evie. But then the last time I felt this way was Sandy and—

Nope. Not going to do it. Not going to let her ruin the best night in ages.

No. *Years.*

Just focus on tonight.

When we arrive at the warehouse, the gamemaster opens the door and lets us inside, his tone that of a clandestine fellow from decades ago. "Hello, my secret agents. Welcome to the 1940s. We have your escape room ready for you."

The gamemaster ushers us down to a basement room, tells us our fellow agents were wrongly taken into police custody, and if we can find the clues and crack the case, we can set them free.

The clock is ticking.

I turn to Olivia. "Do you agree it would be completely embarrassing if we don't find our way out of here? After we both talked about our skill with puzzles?"

"Failure is not an option," she says, her tone intense.

Quickly and methodically, we survey the room. There are wigs, trench coats, mustaches, and maps of the world that look like they belong in an old-time professor's office. A framed portrait hangs behind a large oak desk with a green lamp.

The portrait features a stern-looking man. "His left eye is wonky," I say, pointing to the picture and the way the eye seems askew.

She peers more closely. "It sure is."

She spins around, counting quietly. "And there are nine mirrors in this room."

I catalogue the reflective surfaces—mirrors hanging on walls, one standing on a desk, another next to a globe.

"Mirrors and a wonky eye," I say, tapping my skull.

We spend the next thirty minutes with a laser focus, gathering clues, solving riddles, and cracking codes. We're nearly there. I can feel it. We stand at the desk, poring over one of the last clues, tossing ideas back and forth.

"This is so cool," she says. "If we're good at this, can we make it a thing?"

I laugh, loving that she's already decided we're having another date. "We can definitely make it a thing. We'll tackle all the escape rooms in New York City. How many do you think there are?"

"Thousands," she says softly, tilting her face toward me.

I hold her gaze, not wanting to look anywhere else but into her sparkling blue eyes.

"Olivia," I say, stepping closer to her, a rush of warmth skating over my skin, "are you telling me one hour into this date that you're having such a good time you want to go on a second date?" I don't know why I'm being so forward, yet I know exactly why I'm being so forward. Because she's fascinating. She's interesting. I've never felt this kind of instant, quick, sharp, spicy, tangible connection with somebody. Rather than run away from it, I don't want to let it go.

A lock of her hair is out of place, so I brush it off her shoulder. Her breath seems to hitch. "Yes. I do want to go on another date."

Somewhere in the back of my mind, I'm vaguely

aware of a ticking clock. But I want this more. I run the back of my fingers across her cheek. "Is kissing on your checklist?"

She gasps softly. "I would say kissing *you* is on my checklist, but you have to be a really good kisser to stay on my checklist."

I move my hand to her face, sliding my thumb along her jawline. "It's on mine too."

"Let's check it off." Her eyes flutter shut.

I lean closer to her and brush my lips over hers. I feel a whisper of breath that seems to ghost across her lips, and then the slightest gasp.

She trembles. I'm not even holding her or touching her, I'm just kissing her lightly, softly. And she's shuddering.

It's beautiful and too good to be true.

But it's all true, and it's happening.

She leans into me, inching closer. A soft sigh seems to fall from her lips, a sound that reveals how much she likes this soft, gentle kiss.

I want to know what else makes her feel this way.

I want to be the one to make her feel this way.

The intensity of those twin thoughts shocks me, maybe even scares me a bit, given my past experience.

But everything feels so right about tonight.

And I know that we could easily spend the whole night in here kissing, but I also suspect she'll be ticked if we don't get out of here before the clock.

I separate, even though my skin is buzzing, and my blood is humming. And I'd really like to do that again. Stat.

She blinks. "Wow, now my head is foggy. I don't know if I can concentrate."

"I don't know if I can either. But you know what I like more than kissing you?"

"I can't believe there's anything you like more than kissing me," she pouts.

I loop a hand around her hip, my thumb stroking against her. "I like getting to know you."

She practically purrs. "Herb, let's get the hell out of here, go to a diner, and get to know each other more."

We work, solving the final clue when we position all the mirrors in the room so that they're shining into the portrait's eye. As soon as they do, his eye works like a laser, then opens the door to the escape room.

We laugh and tumble out of the warehouse. The gamemaster tells us that was one of the fastest times that two people have actually executed an escape.

"Guess we had something we wanted outside of the room," I say, glancing at Olivia, who smiles back at me. We want to keep getting to know each other.

I thank the man and turn down the street, reaching for her hand.

She links her fingers through mine.

And am I ever glad I'm moving beyond the past.

Maybe this is insta-like. Heck, maybe it's insta-falling. But screw it. I'm feeling it everywhere.

We wind up at a nearby diner ordering burgers, French fries, and iced tea, and talking. We both agree Madison Square Park is our favorite park in the city, declaring the bench near the MetLife Building a great spot for kissing, then I tell her I like rock, and while she prefers pop, we agree we can coexist on the music front, since everything else is in sync.

Oh, and we also manage to squeeze in some diner kisses. She slides over to my side of the bench, and I wrap an arm around her shoulders, then bring her in close. As kisses go, this one is relatively chaste. We don't want to lose our diner privileges, after all. But the thoughts rushing through my head as I rope my hand in her hair and brush my lips to hers are anything but innocent. When I seal my mouth to Olivia's, I'm not only savoring this connection, I'm imagining where it'll lead to the next time, and the next. I'm picturing more nights, and dates that last well past midnight, and wind up in bed, tangled up together, sheets twisted, skin hot.

And the mornings too.

I'd like to wake up next to her.

I'd like to have breakfast with her.

I'd like to walk her home.

Holy hell, is this insta-something?

I've never been bitten by that bug before, but I'm feeling it now.

This woman and I—we just click.

And I don't want to play games.

We kiss and we chat until we close the place down.

At the end, it feels like we've been on three dates.

"Does this kind of feel like we've already hit the trifecta of three great dates?" I ask.

"It kind of does."

"And each one has been better than the last."

"They're all so good . . . it's almost as if it's too good to be true," she says, her tone light and breezy.

I stop, tug on her hand, and pull her flush against me. "But it's real." My voice is serious.

"It is?" Her tone is pocked with nerves. She looks unsure.

I nod, then cup her cheek and kiss her lips once more, savoring her taste, learning the flavor of her kiss, taking mental snapshots of how she feels in my arms.

Like she's giving herself to me.

And it's entirely what I want.

One freaking date, and I'm sold.

Yup, I've been bitten, and I don't want the antidote. I just want more.

"It's not too good to be true," I say as we break apart.

"Are you sure?" She seems even more flummoxed.

"I'm sure," I say, squeezing her hand. "Besides, who are we to argue with Evie?"

She laughs, but it sounds forced.

"Let me walk you home."

"Okay," she says, her pep and sass nowhere to be found.

That's okay. I'll provide the pep for two.

I take her hand, and along the way, I chat about the city, and the stores we pass.

"That coffee shop has the best vanilla lattes in the city. Don't tell anyone I drink vanilla lattes. But I'm just sharing that tidbit with you," I say, tipping my forehead to a trendy café.

"Oh. Okay."

I blink.

Her tone is . . . *off*.

That's odd.

But I keep going. "Best part of New York," I say, as a man scurries by, arms laden with delivery bags, a stuffed walrus poking out of the top of one, and a plastic robot popping its head from another, "is the delivery anytime anywhere of anything."

"Yes. Definitely."

There it is again.

She drops my hand.

Something shifts in her.

Her stance is stiffer. Her eyes are cooler. Her tone reads distant.

When we reach her place, I squeeze her hand. "You okay? You seem a little off now."

She gives me a huge smile. "I'm great, but I'm so tired, and I need to go. Bye."

She spins around, heads up her steps, and darts inside without a parting glance.

A kiss on the cheek.

Or another word.

I stand on the street wondering how we went from best date ever to what sure looks to turn into a ghosting.

And I've no clue what the hell went wrong.

5

Olivia

Misery is my companion.

It trips me up on the racquetball court the next morning.

With an unladylike grunt, I lunge for the ball, and I smack it wildly. It screams across the court, missing the mark by miles.

Flynn thrusts his arms in victory.

I'm not annoyed he won. I'm simply annoyed. With myself. My thoughts are only on Herb Smith, and how badly I botched last night.

"Rematch?" Flynn asks, eagerness in his eyes.

I don't have the energy to attempt to even the score with my brother. "Nah."

He sets down his racket on the bench. "Clearly something is horribly wrong. Confession time." He pats the wood. "Tell me how you messed up last night."

I can't pretend I didn't. Misery slithers down my spine. "We were having the world's most perfect date," I say, forlorn.

"Yeah, yeah, skip over the sex part."

"We didn't have sex."

"Okay, you didn't have sex, so how could it have been the world's most perfect date?"

I swat him with my towel. "Things do not have to include sex to be awesome."

"But sex does help to make things awesome."

"You know how you didn't want to talk about how I look good in clothes? I don't want to talk about sex with you."

"Okay, fine, so you're having an awesome date." He makes a rolling gesture for me to keep going.

"We hit it off, Flynn. We had insane chemistry. We talked about everything, including how much we liked each other already. That's what freaked me out. We liked each other from the beginning."

His brow knits. "So you're worried it's insta-love?"

"But I don't believe in insta-love."

"Except you felt insta-love for him?" he points out gently.

My stomach flips with the sweetest memories of Herb's kisses, his words, his easy way with me. "I did. That's the thing. I felt insta everything for him." I toss up my hands and look to my brother. "Clearly, there's no way that can work. It's impossible, so I took off at the end."

"That's real mature," he deadpans.

"I couldn't fathom that it was all real . . . And then, what if I'd invited him up?"

"Let's play this game," Flynn says, thoughtful and

logical. "What would have happened? What were you so scared of? Having real feelings for someone you truly like?"

A movie reel plays before my eyes. "I would have had hot, dirty sex with him, and I would have said, 'Let's get married and make babies,' and he'd have said yes, and it would be too good to be true."

"Wait. I thought we weren't supposed to talk about sex. You just said you had hot and dirty sex."

"In my dreams. Yes, it was going to be the hottest sex of my life because I'm that attracted to him. He kissed me in the middle of an escape room, and it was incredible. My toes are still tingling from it. Then he kissed me in the diner and all I saw was a future full of kisses and pancakes and conversations and hot, hot sex."

"This is like immersion therapy or something, right? Where you keep mentioning the deed over and over?"

I grab his arm for emphasis. "Yes, *the deed*. All the deeds. Over and over, but it was more than hot sex and dirty deeds. It was," I stop, remembering how easy everything was with Herb. Every. Single. Thing. "We connected. We hit it off. It was insta-love. And what the hell? That doesn't happen. And if it does, it's dangerous."

"Is it though? Is it dangerous? What if it's the real thing?"

My stomach flutters at the possibility. "It felt like the real thing."

"Why are you standing here with me, then?"

"I don't know. That's a good question." I swallow hard, my throat burning.

He sighs, shaking his head. "Olivia, you're doing it again."

I sigh. I don't fight the truth this time. "I know. I'm sabotaging it. Because I'm afraid."

"And you like this guy. So, woman up and un-sabotage it."

6

Herb

The morning brings no more answers.

Only a gigantic question mark when I check my phone and find zero messages from her.

Then again, I didn't text her either.

I don't need to have her reject me again. Doing it to my face last night was all I needed, thank you very much.

Still, the clinical part of me wants to understand what went down.

As the sun rises, I dribble a basketball on the court in Central Park then send it soaring into the net.

"And then she just left," I tell my buddy Malone, a fellow vet.

"Admittedly, that's not an ideal ending to a date." That's Malone for you. Straight up and to the point. He grabs the ball and whooshes it toward the net.

I snag it on the rebound. "It was literally the definition of a perfect date. Then she said, 'I'm so tired, and I need to go.' Boom. She was gone."

"Ah, now I get it. Sounds like she didn't want to see your sorry ass naked."

I roll my eyes. "My ass is spectacular, clothed or naked."

He shudders, like he's watching a horror flick. "Don't tell me anything more about your ass."

"I'm just saying, it's a gold-standard ass. She was checking it out."

He covers his ears. "Stop. Make it stop."

I shoot the ball, watching it arc into the net. "Anyway, that's that. She made it clear. There's nothing more that's going to happen. I'll just move on."

He grabs the ball, stops, and stares at me. "Wait. That's your takeaway?"

"Well, what should it be?"

"You like this woman, you had a great date, she turned sleepy at the end, and your conclusion is you should just *walk away*?"

"You said sleepy time isn't the ideal ending to a date."

He taps his chest. "I did, and it's not, because sexy time is the ideal ending to a date. But just because you didn't get *there* doesn't mean you stop shooting the basketball."

"I should throw a basketball to get to the sexy times?" I'm thoroughly perplexed.

"No. But here's the thing. You like her, you had chemistry, and you had one weird moment. Dating is weird. It's like when you put a sweater on a cat and they don't know how to walk."

I furrow my brow. "Pretty sure Olivia knows how to walk."

"But you might need to help her take off the sweater."

"Man, your analogy game needs work. Are you saying I need to undress her?"

"No. Well, not yet. But soon. What I am saying is you need to try again."

I crack up, clapping him on the back. "Wow. I didn't get that at all from the cat sweater analogy."

"Just try with her. Give it your best shot. Let her know what you want. The worst that'll happen is you're back out there on the dating circuit, putting sweaters on cats."

Maybe, just maybe, he's right. Maybe I should try to decipher what happened, because that really was the perfect date. And I don't want to give up this time.

7

Olivia

Later that day, I track down my matchmaker. We have lunch, and I tell her what happened.

"I really messed up."

Evie pats my hand. "No, sweetie, you didn't mess up, you got nervous. People get nervous. That's what happens. The question is—where do you go now?"

"I want to see him again. I think he's the one."

She beams. "I believe that too. But you're going to have to make it clear you're not a runner. That you're a stayer. Because I'm pretty sure he wants you to stay."

"Does he?" Tingles sweep through my body.

"The two of you are meant to be."

I quirk an eyebrow. "Do you believe in that? That people are meant to be together?"

"I do. Now you need to do what you should have done last night."

And I don't wait. I whip out my phone at lunch, dial his clinic, and ask to speak to Dr. Smith.

Evie beams the whole time, the proud matchmaker.

"He's with a patient right now. May I take a message?" The man on the other end of the phone asks.

With a smile, and a belly full of nerves, I give him a message. "Can you please tell Dr. Smith that it's Olivia and I would like to know if he would want to work on my checklist at Madison Square Park tonight?"

"I'll give him the message."

Evie claps.

I set down my phone, catching a glimpse of a message icon in the status bar. With butterflies fluttering, I click it open. It arrived fifteen minutes ago.

Herb: Hey, Olivia, so I'm not really sure what went wrong last night, but I'd like to try again with you. If you're up for it, maybe we can meet at Madison Square Park after work.

He must have sent it before I even called him. Oh God, I think I'm falling in love. My fingers speed through the fastest reply in the world.

Olivia: YES!!!!!! I'm there!

* * *

We arrive at the same time.

He walks toward me. I walk toward him. I stop in front of the bench, nerves and hope clogging my throat.

"I'm sorry I freaked out last night."

He sits and I sit next to him. "Are you a runner? Because once I have you as mine, I'm not going to want you to run away."

I take a deep breath. "I had a bad relationship. He cheated on me with a ton of other people, and sometimes I sabotage dates when it seems like it might work. I especially do when it's too good to be true."

He smiles and runs his thumb over my jawline. "So you think I'm too good to be true?"

"You said it yourself last night. Everything seemed that way."

"And that scared you?"

"It did. But that's no excuse." I reach for his hand. When he threads his fingers through mine, I swear all is right in the world. "Maybe it's too soon. Maybe it's too much. But I want to know what we can be."

He sighs, but it sounds like it's full of happy relief. "Look, I was hurt too. I was in love with this woman, and she took off around the world. I keep waiting for someone to pull the rug out from under me again."

My heart aches for him. "I don't want to pull the rug out from under you."

He sweeps his thumb over my jaw. "And I don't want to hurt you. All I want is to make you feel good."

And my heart—it soars to the sky. "That's the past. This is the present." I smile, and the way he smiles back at me, all crooked and sexy, sends heat through my body.

"There's only one way to find out if this thing is too good to be true," he says, his voice low, husky. His hand slinks around my neck, into my hair, sending shivers down my spine.

"To do this thing."

"Let's do this thing." He dips his face to my neck

then kisses me there. "You know what escape room I'd like to go to right now?"

"Which one?" I'm trembling with desire.

"There's one in my apartment."

I moan. "If you take me there, I'm not going to want to escape."

"That's the plan."

I plant a kiss on his lips, and it's better than last night. It's wonderful and magical, and I feel it everywhere. Everything else fades away but the absolute magic of this man and me. Maybe I'm crazy, but I swear I can taste forever in his kiss.

I make a choice.

To break my habits and make brand new ones.

Starting with the hot, dirty sex I'd hoped for.

Funny, how a man so sweet can be so dirty in the sack. Because when we make it to my apartment, the alpha animal in him comes out. And my sweet, swoony vet is whispering filthy things in my ear.

Things like . . .

Want to strip off all your clothes.

Spread you out on the bed.

Eat you, taste you, have you.

Fuck you.

Fuck you so damn hard you're not just seeing stars, but planets and galaxies.

Who knew that Herb Smith had such a dirty mouth?

"You are quite naughty," I say, shuddering as I grab his shirt, tugging it over his head as we stumble to my bed.

"I am. And hey, maybe that is what makes me too good to be true."

I laugh as I drag my nails down the grooves in his abs. *Grooves.* The man has traceable grooves. "Yes, definitely too good, because I do like it when you tell me all the bad things you want to do."

He yanks off my top, unclasps my bra, and dips his head to my breasts, murmuring as he licks a circle around my nipple. "I'd like to lick, and kiss, and fuck you all night long, Olivia. Take you hard, take you slow, take you every way."

I shiver. Is he for real? Is this happening?

My knees shake and I gasp as he lavishes attention on my breasts, telling me how delicious my skin is, how good I taste, how he could spend the night worshipping my body.

Yes.

I'd like that very much.

But I want to worship his too. And even when he has me squirming and panting, I don't let my own pleasure deter me. I sit up, pressing a hand to his chest.

"Let me taste you."

He arches a brow, his eyes darkening. "Yeah?"

"Let me show you how much I want you too."

"Show me," he says, more commanding than I expected.

He wraps my hair in a fist, and tugs me down to him. I'm hot and bothered and so ready for all sorts of dirty deeds as I take him in my mouth.

He moans and groans, muttering *just like that, yeah, deeper, your mouth feels so damn good, so fucking good*, that I swear I'm going to orgasm from his words. His reaction. His *realness*.

When his words turn into nonsense, he pulls me up, brings me close, and whispers *let me fuck you now, sweetheart.*

And yep. I'm done for. That's it. I'm gone. It's insta-lust, insta-love, insta-everything.

The deed is spectacular. It's electric and intense, it's

wild and frenzied, it's slow and tender. It's the best it's ever been.

But it's not too good to be true. It's better.

I suppose that's how it goes when you've finally met the man who ticks all the boxes and then some.

* * *

Herb

The next morning I take her out for pancakes.

With her fork in hand, she dives in with gusto. "I love pancakes."

"Some people do."

"Hey! Don't rain on my pancake parade." She eyes my plate of eggs. "Why didn't you order pancakes?"

I sigh heavily and level with her. "I don't like them."

Her blue eyes pop. "What? How is that possible?"

"Just don't. I'm an eggs and hash browns kind of guy."

She shakes her head vehemently. "I refuse to believe anyone can dislike pancakes."

I tap my chest. "This guy does."

She huffs, takes another bite of her pancakes, then smiles. "Herb." She sets down her fork and gives me a strange smile.

"What? Is this a deal-breaker? A new act of sabotage?"

She stands, moves around the table, and sits down next to me, then kisses my cheek. "You told me you hate pancakes, and I still like you. This must be the real thing."

I laugh, cup her cheek, and bring her close for another kiss.

"And amazingly, I can tolerate the taste of pancakes on your lips."

She tap-dances her fingers down my shirt. "I'll get you to like them eventually."

"We'll see about that."

I walk her home, and outside her apartment she gives me the best redo ever—kissing the hell out of me and making me wish I could take the rest of the day off.

Instead, I peel myself away, send her a text, and ask if I can see her that night.

Seconds later, she replies with a yes.

It's possible I send her a few more texts that day. It's possible some are sweet. It's possible some are dirty too. She seems to like all those sides of me, and hell, I like all of hers.

Or really, *love* is the better word.

EPILOGUE

Olivia

I spend the night. And the next night, and the next one, and the next one.

For several wonderful blissful months that culminate in a ring, a promise, and a shared home.

Right now, I'm heading to meet Evie to thank her for setting me up with the man who has become my fiancé. When I see her at the coffee shop, Flynn is with her. "If we could only convince Flynn to let me work on him," Evie says, crossing her fingers.

He shakes his head. "Nope. I'm too focused on work."

I shoot him a *you're so ridiculous* look, then turn to Evie. "Someday he'll realize there is a meant-to-be for him, since I found mine. And we're going to Bora Bora for our honeymoon."

Flynn's green eyes light up. "He passed the Bora Bora litmus test."

"And someday you'll find someone who passes yours," I say.

My brother might be reluctant, he might have his own reasons for keeping up his guard, but I believe that deep down, there's a woman who's going to be his perfect match.

I found mine.

I thought he was too good to be true.

Then I realized that some things simply are, and those are the ones you don't let slip away.

THE END

Intrigued by Flynn? He has his own story to tell in COME AS YOU ARE, the smash hit romance that'll have you swooning, out now! Malone's story is told in SATISFACTION GUARANTEED, available everywhere!

STRONG SUIT

A short story

ABOUT

From the day I meet Ginny in the conference room, I'm smitten with the co-worker who's ten years my senior. And I'm going to pull out all the stops to win her over.

HER PROLOGUE

A year ago

For the record, I did not—underline *not*—make the offer because he's hot.

I *only* made the offer because I'm helpful.

That was it.

That was all.

It went down like this.

At the end of a department-head meeting, my boss popped in, introduced the new director of sales, then— because he had an unexpected meeting with a client— asked if someone wouldn't mind showing him around.

Wouldn't mind?

Ah, hell no.

Because Noah Rivera was easy on the eyes.

And had the best smile ever.

But wait. That's not why I stuck my hand in the air.

"I'll be happy to show him around," I offered.

I did it because I liked to help.

Always had, always would.

"Why, thank you very much for being my tour guide," Noah said as we walked down the hall and I showed him the food labs at our chocolate company.

"I like to wear all sorts of hats. Head of marketing, captain of the softball team, and chief tour guide."

He stopped in his tracks. "Whoa. Did you just say softball team?"

I laughed. "Yes. Is that a surprise?"

"No. It's just—could this day get any better? I love softball."

I nudged his elbow.

Wait, did I just nudge his elbow?

Must behave.

I tried to make light of it. "Then you really ought to join our team. We have a ton of fun playing with the other food companies in the city."

He shot me a quizzical look. "And you like sports leagues? Like, really like them?"

"Sure. My daughter's school is right near the park, so it works out perfectly. She'll meet me at Central Park and work on homework during the games."

His eyes swept down to my hand. Was he hunting for a ring? Well, he wouldn't find one.

"That is so cool that you're into—I mean, that Heavenly has a softball team. I'm fired up to join."

I flashed him a smile. "And I'm fired up you want to join."

I gave him the rest of the tour, popping by to say hi to other key team members, saving the best for last.

When we reached the corporate cafeteria, I swept my arm out wide. "And the best part? Heavenly has fabulous food. Yummy soups and delicious salads, and all sorts of options if you're a vegetarian or gluten-free, or what have you."

He nodded appreciatively at the spread. "This is going to be perfect."

I glanced at my watch. It was twelve thirty.

"Want to get something to eat?"

He smiled brightly. "Is everyone here as friendly as you?"

I shrugged playfully. "We do have a great group of people. That's why I've been here for more than a decade." I lowered my voice to a conspiratorial whisper. "Not for nothing, they do call me Ambassador Ginny."

He offered a hand. "Have I mentioned what a pleasure it is to meet you, Ambassador Ginny?"

"And it's a pleasure to meet you, Noah."

See, I did all that because I'm helpful.

Not because I was totally perving on the hot new guy.

We sat down and had lunch together, and that's when I made the biggest mistake.

"Tell me more about you."

I learned he lived in Queens, a few blocks from his family, had dinner with his parents every Sunday, and liked to play soccer with his older sister's youngest son.

He was a freaking twenty-five-year-old family man.

Thanks, universe, for the temptation.

HIS PROLOGUE

She was friendly. Outgoing. Liked softball. Could talk up a storm.

She was also sexy as hell.

Oh, and she had an Australian accent.

Nothing hotter in all the world.

It was official.

I was falling in love.

1
_____

Noah

I hear my favorite sound when I head to the break room to grab a bottle of water. The sound of a certain woman.

"You know how it is, right?"

That sexy voice. Gets me every time. In the you-know-where.

Ginny is pouring a cup of coffee and talking to a gal who works in operations. "I hear ya," the woman, Julie, says.

"You're just so overwhelmed, you try to do two things at once all the time, like you suddenly think you're super-woman, and you can both wash dishes and dry them at the same time."

Julie chuckles. "Or fold laundry at the exact moment that you're cooking."

"What a skill set. Don't I wish I could do that."

"I'd also like to be able to sleep and exercise simulta-neously."

Ginny high-fives Julie. "That's how it is being a mom. You're completely convinced you can do everything, and then you get really cocky, and also totally overwhelmed, so you try to do two diametrically opposed things at once that never work. Like brush your teeth and pee."

"Girl, that never works."

"Which leads me to my point. All this superwoman stuff—we can have it all—is just a bunch of poppycock. We're simply trying to do it all, and we fail at all the things that way. For instance, how can I truly do one of the gazillion things on my to-do list while I'm working out? Too hard to answer email. Can't fold laundry and exercise. And I've yet to figure out how to sweep the floors while I'm on the treadmill."

I figure this is my chance to cut in since working out is my hobby, my passion, my second favorite physical activity. I turn the corner into the room. "You could try doing squats while you brush your teeth," I offer in as friendly a way as possible. "After all, isn't that a great use of time? That's totally achievable. I do that every day, in fact. I always do squats and lunges while I brush my teeth, and I use my electric toothbrush, which runs for a full two minutes. You do thirty seconds on each quadrant of your mouth, so I do lunges on each side. Right, left, right, left, boom, done."

I do a few squats and a couple of lunges to demonstrate.

The redhead, oh the glorious, gorgeous redhead Ginny—who's become a colleague, a teammate, a friend, and a lunch companion, which is thoroughly awesome because lunch is one of my three favorite meals, the others being breakfast and dinner—stares at me curiously, her lips quirking up.

"Are you saying I need to do squats, Noah?"

I gulp. I did not mean to insult her at all. All I want is to shower her with compliments. "No, your legs are—"

"You think I'm not working out enough?"

Abort, abort, abort.

I grab the steering wheel of the plane, and I try to fly it out of the crash landing that I'm about to careen into.

The last thing I want is for the woman I'm totally hot for to think she's anything less than a ten. No, a one hundred. No, a one thousand on the scale of total freaking gorgeousness, charm, and personality.

She's the warmest, friendliest gal I've ever met and has been since day one. If I could just figure out how to get her to see me in a new way.

I point furiously at the legs in question. "No, God no. Your legs are toned, tanned, and perfect."

I mentally slap myself upside the head. Am I allowed to say that in the workplace? I have no idea what I'm allowed to do in the workplace anymore.

Julie snickers. "I feel like it might be my cue to go. Seems you two have a lot of multitasking and exercise life hacks to chat about."

She exits as Ginny arches a brow and says, "I'll have you know, I do try to do squats, because they are good for your legs."

"They're great for your legs. I pray at the altar of squats every single day."

She taps her chin. "But I did kind of think"—Ginny drops her voice to a naughty whisper—"that squats were good for your butt . . ." She trails off, her eyes drifting as if she's checking out her own rear end. Oh, I would like to be looking out of her sockets right now and staring at her fine ass. Not that I haven't checked out her cheeks every single time she strolls down the hall. Yes, I like her personality, but I dig her looks too.

A lot.

I'm confident, though, that I can't compliment her butt. That's definitely not cool in the workplace.

"Your legs . . ."

Hold on. I don't know if I'm even allowed to say her legs are perfect. Is that verboten? What the hell am I allowed to say to a woman I work with anymore? We're lateral here at Heavenly. It's not like I'm her boss or vice versa, but I don't know if I'm allowed to hit on a woman at work.

"My legs are strong," she says with a smile, finishing my half-said sentence. "I live in a fifth-floor walk-up, so I've already managed to combine exercise and transportation. See, that's the one thing I have mastered multitasking."

I breathe a sigh of relief. We're on the same wavelength, so I decide to push a little further past the work zone. "Well, that's awesome. Also, aren't electric toothbrushes good for, ya know, other things?"

Her grin is the definition of wicked. "Noah, are you about to say something vastly inappropriate about electric toothbrushes?"

"I don't know what I possibly could have been saying," I say, as cheeky and innocent as possible.

She steps closer, her eyes tap-dancing with delight. "Were you going to say that using an electric toothbrush is a euphemism for using something else?"

I part my lips to speak when she flashes me a smile, presses a finger to her lips, and says, "We'll just pretend neither one of us mentioned battery-operated devices."

She exits in a cloud of honeysuckle copper hair and

an Aussie accent that turns me all the way on. And yes, as she walks down the hall, I watch her walk away.

Someday, someday soon, I'm going to come up with a proper plan for how to woo Ginny Perretti.

2

Ginny

Groan.

Epic groan.

Absolutely epic groan worthy of a meme.

What was I thinking?

It's a question I write in my idea notebook in big, blocky letters. Then, because I want to make sure I remember it, I do a 3-D outline of the block letters.

What were you thinking, self?

I can't lead him on. Even though, my God, he is one of the cutest men I have ever seen. Cute as in red-hot, want to jump him, sexy as sin. But he's a boy, that's what I have to remind myself.

He's twenty-freaking-five.

What the hell would I do with a twenty-five-year-old? What would we talk about?

The same things you have been talking about.

I tell that voice to shut up.

Because those arms, that face, that dusting of scruff. The whole picture of Noah Rivera is everything I shouldn't want.

You don't need a younger man.

I write it again.

And again.

And again.

I shift gears from my reminder, scrawling out my ideas for our next marketing campaign, repeating silently, *He's too young for me.*

That's the trouble.

I've always been drawn to younger guys, and they're always dangerous. They're not serious, they don't have their act together, they don't know how to take care of you. Even though I absolutely do not, in any way, shape, or form need a man to take care of me, I *do* need someone I don't have to mother.

I'm thirty-five and I have a ten-year-old daughter. I'm a single mom, and I've only ever been a single mom.

My daughter's father left me before she was born, and I raise her all by myself. That's why I don't need yet another young guy in my life, someone who can't compute what it's like to have responsibilities. After all, he's the man who has enough free time to train for marathons, play in the company softball league, do a kickass amazing job as the director of sales, *and* probably get a full night's rest too. He might be exceedingly excellent at playing the Uncle Noah role, but c'mon. As endearing as that is, it's not the same as actually having everyday responsibilities of the permanent kind. I have to remind myself of that every time I feel tempted.

My boss taps the door to my office. "Idea," he announces.

I turn around and wave at the man the other ladies

call Mr. Tall, Dark, and Handsome. They might as well add "Unavailable" to his business card, because Leo wears unattainable like a cologne. Works for me, since we're friends and only ever will be buds. I have this crazy hunch he's still carrying a torch for a woman from his past, but he doesn't like to talk about mushy stuff, so I don't prod too much about the woman named Lulu. A woman I've noticed him looking at pictures of on his phone now and then. "Hey, Leo. What ideas are rattling around in that big old brain of yours?"

He strokes his chin. "What's rattling is this. The Big Chocolate Show is coming up soon." He wiggles his eyebrows. "Are you thinking what I'm thinking?"

I raise my hand like I have the answer in class. "That we're going to gorge ourselves on chocolate to successfully achieve the nirvana state known as a chocolate coma?"

He taps his skull. "You can indeed read my mind. Because I do fully expect us to sample as much as we possibly can."

I pat my stomach. "I'm in. I'm awesome at chocolate sampling. You ever need help with that, you call on me."

"You're the only one I would ever call on." He clears his throat. "But in all seriousness, what I was really thinking was at the show we should look for the next rising star."

I bounce on my toes at the prospect of finding a top chocolatier to design a line of craft chocolates for Heavenly. "Yes, that was actually the real mind meld that I was receiving from you. Brilliant idea, and I'm going to be on the lookout."

That's what I focus on this afternoon: devising a strategy for the upcoming trade show. I don't at all think about the young, sexy, muscular, perfect-bodied, Michael

Peña look-alike who tried to make *an electric toothbrush is like a vibrator* joke.

I might, though, use one of those devices tonight while thinking about him—and it's definitely not the electric toothbrush.

The next day, in the break room, I find Noah digging into a kale salad.

That's a sign right there. I despise kale, and Noah likes it.

All I have to do is focus on things I dislike, and I'll get rid of my desire for him.

I mime gagging.

3

Noah

I take the bait.

"Hmm. I get the feeling you're trying to say you don't like kale? Is that what you're saying, Ginmeister?"

She rolls her eyes. "Noah, no one likes kale."

I stand tall and proud in front of the podium in kale defense. "Not true. I love it, love it, love it. Like adore it. I think it's one of the greatest foods ever."

She shoots me a skeptical look. "That's not possible."

"No, it is possible. See?" I take another bite and I chew, smiling and humming as I go. Oh, that was a bit of a mistake, because kale definitely takes a couple of years to chew through, and that's going to make it harder for me to talk, and talking is absolutely one of my strong suits when it comes to Ginny. Except it's also my wild card still, because what if I say something that turns her off? Screw it. I'm the eternal optimist, so I choose to believe everything will all be good. "I love kale, and I bet you can too."

"But you're a health nut," she says. "That means you have to love it."

"By virtue of being a card-carrying eater of veggies and protein?"

"Yes, you're a flag-waving member."

"Ha, you said 'member.'"

She laughs.

Like I said, the mouth is a wild card. "And kale is delicious."

"Maybe to someone who never eats chocolate," she suggests, her brow furrowing. God, she's adorable when she argues. She gets a little crinkle between her eyebrows that I want to run my finger over, that I want to press my lips against, that I want to kiss.

And I officially have it bad for this woman if the crinkle in her forehead gets me excited. "I bet you've never had a roasted sesame seed kale salad, have you?"

She pretends to wretch.

"How about kale mixed with brussels sprouts and lemon?"

She clutches her stomach. "Are you trying to make it sound as awful and miserable as possible?"

I laugh. "Ginny, you don't know what you're missing." *When it comes to kale and men.*

"I am definitely not missing kale."

I set down my salad bowl, reach for her arm, and wrap my hand around it. She's quiet at first, and so am I, because, hello, did I just kind of make a move by touching her arm? And does it actually feel better than how a hand wrapped around an arm should feel?

She lets her eyes drift to my palm, and I swear she trembles slightly, a little shudder that makes me think she likes it when I touch her. Makes me want to go for it with her. It emboldens me.

"Let me make you a kale treat," I say in my best sexy voice.

She smiles softly. Kind of sexy. A little sweet too. As I let go of her arm, her fingers trail down my wrist.

Holy kale smoothie, she *is* flirting with me, and I have a leafy vegetable to thank.

She pins her gaze on me, her eyes fierce, her expression playful. "Bring it on, Noah Rivera."

There. Right there. When a woman uses your full name, it's definitely a sign. A sign of something good.

So I keep it up. No need to stop the volley now. "And if I prove you like kale? What then? What happens if I win the great kale battle?"

"It's a contest?"

"Hell yeah. Contests are awesome."

She laughs. "Fine. If I win, you have to make my next PowerPoint."

I scoff. She probably thinks it's a punishment. Little does she know nothing gets me down, not even Power-Points. I'm actually ridiculously good at them, and I tell her as much.

"Ginny, I'm the master of PowerPoints. You can count me in."

"The master of PowerPoints, you say? Tell me what other talents you have. Can you fold laundry?"

I puff out my chest. "I can fold laundry, I can do my own laundry. I'm fully house-trained," I pause, then add, "in chores."

"Stop, Noah, you're getting me excited." Excited is exactly where I want her.

"Chores get you excited?"

"Chores are the way to my heart."

I decide to nudge open that door, leaning on my sexiest voice. "Would you let me do some chores for you?"

She waves her hand in front of her chest, like she's heating up. "Please. You can't say such seductive things in the office," she whispers.

Then I kick the door, as if I'm doing just that. Seducing her. "Cleaning dishes. Mopping floors. Sweeping, dusting, even . . ." I pause, take a beat. "Vacuuming."

She lets out a gasp, like I've hit the jackpot.

Then she schools her expression. "Anyway, enough about chores. I do have to go back to my desk and I can't very well spend the whole afternoon thinking about *chores*, can I?"

This woman. Damn. I want her. "I don't see the problem with that. But what do I get if I win?"

She tilts her chin, like she's thinking. Her eyes flicker, the hint of a smile in them. "What do you want?"

I strip away the teasing for a split second, dead serious. "I think you know what I want."

She swallows, looks away, then back at me, vulnerability in her eyes. "I do." And her expression and tone shift once more to flirty. "How about you get the *satisfaction* of me liking kale?"

Now that, that is definitely flirting. And I'm fully satisfied.

That night, after I run ten miles and do a full circuit of weights at the gym, I research the best kale salads in New York City, because no way am I fucking this up by making it on my own.

The next morning, on the way to work, I stop at a gourmet shop that is purported to have an incredible kale salad with sesame.

At the office later, I find her in the cafeteria and offer it to her for lunch.

She arches a skeptical brow. "I won't like this."

"I know. You won't like it. You'll *love* it."

She takes a forkful, chews, then stares daggers at me. "You tricked me."

I smile. "No trickery."

"This is bloody delicious."

"I told you so."

"But there's no way you can top this."

"I so can."

"Why do you like healthy food so much? And exercise?"

"Why? Because I want to live a long, healthy life, have a couple kids, and be around to play soccer with their grandkids too. That's why."

Her eyes flicker with something new, something I haven't seen in them before. "Is that so?"

Her tone is a little less of the usual flirty and sarcastic. It's almost like it's been stripped bare.

"That is very much so."

Her friend Julie joins her, so I return to my table. But I decide to have some more fun with the redhead, since she seems to like it so much. I ask the guy next to me for a sheet of paper from his notebook and a pen. I write in the middle of the paper. Then I fold it, give it some wings, and send it to her at her table. I watch as it soars, landing gently on Ginny's tray of pasta.

She seems surprised at first, then she looks up and notices me. I shoot her a grin. She smiles right back, and it sure looks as if she digs that I sent her this. That I'm not an annoyance to her, that she's getting quite the little kick out of this strange flirtation.

When she unfolds the wings, she grins. That sexy

kind of smile. A little bit wicked, a little bit mischievous, something that tells me that maybe there are tingles running through her body.

God knows I have way more than tingles—I've got a whole lot of lust rattling through me as I savor the view of Ginny Perretti opening my paper airplane and reading my note.

"Satisfaction is coming."

4

Ginny

I shouldn't have touched his arm in the break room.

But who can blame me?

The man is hella toned. His body is like a work of exercise art.

Honestly, though, that's not his biggest selling feature. I'd still like him if he was soft in the middle.

Noah Rivera piques my interest for many other reasons. His persistence. His oddball humor. His zest for, well, everything.

His big, crazy heart. My God, the man wants to have kids and grandkids, and wants to play with them.

This is not fair.

Still, I need to resist hot young things. I've been down this road before, and I don't know that I want to travel it again and take a chance at being left high and dry.

After I put my daughter to bed, I vow not to text him.

Don't respond to his paper airplane message.

That's what I've been trying to do all afternoon. All evening.

Don't respond, don't give in, don't do it.

Two hours of Netflix bingeing later, I'm still resisting him.

Though I have given in to my third glass of wine, turned on the scalding hot water in the tub, and run a bubble bath.

Calgon, take me away.

I sink down under the water with my phone on the ledge of the tub. One more sip of chardonnay.

I picture Noah. Wonder what he's up to. I linger on that word. *Satisfaction.* And as the water slip-slides around my naked body, I feel my resistance tiptoe out the door.

Ginny: Satisfaction is coming? You don't say. All from more kale?

Noah: It was delicious, wasn't it?

Ginny: I'll admit it was quite tasty. Just as I said earlier.

Noah: Wait till tomorrow. I'll have something even better for you.

Ginny: Something better, you say?

Noah: Does that pique your interest?

I put my phone down so I don't reply with something naughty like, say, *You pique all sorts of parts.*

Just to be safe, I set the phone on the bath mat so I'm not tempted. But as I sink under the water, I replay our flirtations, our break room bump-ins, the little touches, and the paper airplane.

My skin heats up, and it's not from the water in the tub. It's from the way he flirts with me, and from the way I like it more than I want to.

5

Noah

The next day, I do it again. I find another shop, and I bring her another kale treat. I hand it to her in the break room.

"What's this?" she asks, as if she can't possibly believe it could be food. She holds it between her fingers.

I adopt my most serious tone. "We call that chocolate-covered kale."

She coughs. "Seriously? Are you trying to turn me off?"

Ah, hell. I just can't resist. I step closer. "No, I'm trying to turn you on. Don't you get that by now?"

She doesn't say anything at first, and I freeze, worried I've crossed a line. But she dips a toe over it, whispering, "Are you?"

"I definitely am." I take a beat. "So, is it working?"

She holds up a thumb and forefinger. "A little."

And I can work with *a little*. I can definitely work with that. "Excellent."

"Just promise me you won't ever bring me a kale smoothie."

I raise my right hand. "I'm taking an oath. I'm not that cruel. But chocolate-covered kale is another story. Why don't you try it?"

She takes a bite, considering. "What do you know? I don't think that's half bad."

I pump a fist. "I knew I could convert you."

She arches a brow. "I'm not totally converted. Now, in the future if you want to spoil me, chocolate and wine are the way to go."

I pretend to type. "Filing that away."

Leo strolls by, and I straighten. So does Ginny, almost as if we've done something wrong, and we don't want the boss man to catch us.

I choose to take that as another good sign, so much that I drop off a square of chocolate on her desk before I leave. That night while I'm at the gym, she texts me.

Ginny: Now that was even better than the chocolate-covered kale.

Noah: Excellent. Did you finish all of it?

Ginny: I did finish it. I'm quite good at finishing.

Oh, that's definitely a dirty euphemism.

Noah: I'm quite good at finishing too.

Ginny: What are you good at finishing?

Noah: Whatever I set my mind to. I have excellent stamina. I've finished marathons. I've finished races. I can finish whatever I need to finish.

Ginny: I love finishing.

And I'm on fire. Because she is almost certainly, most definitely, 100 percent all but sexting with me.

Noah: What are you going to finish right now?

Ginny: I'm having a soak in the tub.

Noah: You're a mermaid, yowza. Do you have a bath bomb?

Ginny: I bow to the inventor of bath bombs.

Noah: Favorite kind?

Ginny: Honeysuckle.

Noah: Of course. And you smell like honeysuckle.

Ginny: You've been sniffing me?

No point lying now, so I tap out a reply as I climb the StairMaster.

Noah: Yes. You smell incredible. Your scent is the perfect finishing touch.

Ginny: All this talk of finishing reminds me that I ought to finish this bath.

Noah: And after that, will you finish other things?

Ginny: It seems possible.

I stare at the phone as I climb, sweat slinking down my brow. Holy shit. She's a dirty girl.

We've jumped from electric toothbrushes to kale to wine to bath dirty talk, and I want to go over to her place right now and get in the tub with her, and I don't even like baths. I mean, come on, baths are kind of dirty.

I'm a shower guy. But a bath with Ginny Perretti? Hell yeah.

6

Ginny

The next day I bang my head against the desk.

Must. Stop. Flirting.

I absolutely must. What is wrong with me?

I can't believe I got that bawdy last night. I can't even blame the wine. Because I know better. I was supposed to focus on arguing with Noah, finding things I dislike, reasons we wouldn't work, and instead I flirted with him yet again. I write my mantra down in my notebook.

Must. Stop. Flirting.

But I don't follow my own commands.

I keep arguing with him, like when I see him in the break room over the next week, and we debate who the best Bond is.

I say Pierce Brosnan, he insists on Daniel Craig.

We discuss when mason jars became okay for pretty much everything, and then we talk about murses. I don't mind them, but he says no man should ever carry one.

And he sends me more paper airplanes. Sometimes he writes funny words in them. Sometimes he'll suggest a random topic he wants to debate the next day—why does honey belong in mustard but not ketchup?—and other times his paper airplanes are a little flirty.

Every day, though, I find myself looking forward to these moments, and at the same time, I remind myself that getting involved with a young guy from work would be a huge mistake, and I don't have room to make any.

* * *

A few days later, I stop by my boss's office before I leave for the day. "I'm all ready for the show this weekend. We'll go searching for our star."

In a split second, he closes his laptop. For a moment I wonder if he was looking at pictures of that woman again. He turns his gaze away from the machine, and Leo leans back in his chair. "I have my treasure map. I'm ready."

I thrust a fist in the air. "We won't leave until we track him or her down."

"We will be victorious."

"Of course we will."

As luck would have it, we do find a promising prospect at the chocolate show, a lovely, friendly, wildly outgoing woman with crazy curly hair, bright blue shoes, and a big personality. I hit it off with her instantly then learn something extraordinary.

She extends a hand. "Lulu Diamond."

Ohhhhhhh.

Well.

That's rather interesting.

She's the woman from Leo's past.

She's the one I'd bet a lifetime of chocolate he still carries a torch for, even if he'd deny it under oath or severe tickling.

But requited or unrequited love isn't for me to weigh in on.

"Ginny Perretti. Pleasure to meet you."

She glances at my jewelry, a heart-shaped necklace my daughter gave me. "I love your necklace, and you have the best hair."

I pat my red locks. "And you're perfect. You're hired. For anything and everything."

"Excellent. I'll be there tomorrow morning at nine a.m. on the dot."

I decide I love her, and I'm pretty sure I want her to be my new best friend.

That's one more reason I'm glad my company chooses her as our next rising star chocolatier.

But the weird thing is, when I sit down for lunch at the cafeteria a few weeks later and see she's chatting with Noah at the salad bar, a small nugget of jealousy digs into me. I'm almost embarrassed that I'm the least bit envious.

I like Lulu. I consider her a fast friend, and I don't want to feel so green, especially since nothing has happened with Noah.

I remind myself that Noah's friendly, he talks to everybody. So when Lulu sits down with me to dine, I shove thoughts of him away once again.

That's truly becoming my top sport—denying my desire for the hot young guy who's become so much more than that. He's become the man I'm interested in. Very, very interested in. Because this hot young guy is so good, and honorable. It's not him, it's me—my past makes me want to be very, very cautious.

"I'm so glad it's you who's the rising star," I say.

"Well, I'm glad it's me too," she says.

"We need more chicks here at the office."

"Girl power. I'm all for that."

As we chat about her plans for the new line of choco-late, something whooshes over my head. A paper airplane lands in front of my tray, and a rush of heat spreads across my chest. "Noah," I say, rolling my eyes to deflect but unable to hold in a smile.

"Noah sends you paper airplanes?"

I pick up the winged object. "He likes to send these to me at lunch. He's such a goofball."

"Regularly? He sends them regularly?"

"Once or twice a week."

"Pretty sure that means he's into you."

I try to dismiss the idea, even though I know he is. But if I give in to it, I'll give in to him. And it's too soon. "Oh, no. He's just . . . festive."

Lulu glances behind her, and Noah waves to me. "No. I think he has a thing for you. A big thing. The look on his face seems to say it all. What about you? Is it mutual?"

I've been storing all my worries inside me, and at last I have the chance to talk them through. I blurt out, "I'm thirty-five. I'm ten years older than he is. Is that terrible?"

"Only if you let it be terrible. But your face says you like him too."

My stomach swoops. What am I going to do about all these butterflies? What am I going to do about Noah?

I look over at him, taking in his handsome face, his golden skin, his dark hair, and his smile. I don't even want to admit it to myself, much less to her, but I think I need to.

"Maybe I do," I say, since the truth feels better.

"Maybe someday, then, for the two of you."

"Maybe someday," I echo.

After Lulu leaves, Noah walks over, clears his throat, and hands me a paper airplane.

This one seems different than all the others, but the trouble is I don't know if I'm ready yet to set aside my rules.

Even though I find myself wanting to more every day I spend around him.

7

Noah

Do it now.

A voice in the back of my head repeats: *Do it now. Just go for it. Ask Ginny out this weekend. Ask her out for lunch. Ask her out for coffee. Ask her out for a glass of wine. Ask her to go bath-bomb shopping. Ask her out to taste-test kale salad anywhere. Take your chance.*

This time I listen to the voice, writing on the paper airplane, then personally delivering it as we leave the cafeteria together.

She opens it as we walk, reading the words I wrote.

"Someday I'd like to take you out."

Her eyes meet mine, and hers seem to sparkle with a little bit of hope, maybe even possibility. "You would?"

I keep going for it. "I would. What would you say if I asked you?"

She nibbles on her lip, sighing.

That's when I remind myself that love is a marathon,

it's not a sprint. I press my hand over hers. "Don't give me an answer now."

"Why do you say that?" she asks curiously.

"Because there is only one answer I want."

A smile seems to sneak across her face. "What is the answer you want?"

"The *only* answer I want is yes."

Her smile stretches further. "And you think I'm going to give you a yes?"

"I'm an optimist. Optimism is my strong suit. Maybe even my strongest."

"That's a good strong suit to have."

"It is," I agree, since it's what's going to fuel me as I run this marathon with Ginny. "Now isn't the time. But someday it's going to be a yes."

"Someday you say?" She's smiling wider now.

"What do you think, Ginny?" I ask as we reach the stairwell. "Will it be someday?"

"Maybe," she says, and we're getting closer.

"Excellent. You think I can get you from a maybe to a yes soon?"

She shrugs, a little playfully. "I think maybe if you try hard enough, you just might do that."

"I can do that. I can definitely do that."

She dusts invisible lint off my shoulder. "Go for it, Noah Rivera. Wear me down."

The die has been cast, the gauntlet has been thrown, and I make it my mission to wear her down, but in, you know, a positive way, the way we both want.

The next week, as we embark on a crazy corporate scavenger hunt across New York, I work my magic.

After we solve the first clue and our teammates go off to check out a traveling exhibit, I seize my first shot at wearing her down on the steps of the Met, thanks to carbs.

I shudder at the thought of carbs when Ginny points to a pretzel cart. "I'm hungry. I think I'll grab a pretzel."

But if pretzels ring her bell, so be it. I swivel around. "Pretzels are on me," I offer.

Her lips hook into a smile. "But it's not a date." She says it a little flirty, like she's making her point, but also leaving the door open.

"I know. It's only pretzels. I can buy the *only pretzels* though," I say, because this is progress.

"But it's not a date for these *only pretzels*," she repeats.

"Someday it will be."

Ginny shakes her head, but she's smiling. "And that someday, it won't be pretzels." She arches an eyebrow in a naughty little wiggle that reminds me of our *finishing* chats.

I pump a fist. "We'll start with a snack and work up to a *someday*."

"Yes, let's start with pretzels and see where we finish."

Oh yeah, even with carbs, this is getting good.

* * *

The next day we're working the clue at Washington Square Park, trying to figure out where it'll take us, when

Ginny yawns. "Sorry, guys. I'm a bit off my game. Had a late night with my daughter."

"Is everything okay with her?" I ask.

Ginny smiles, and it's a new kind of grin, proud and maternal. "She's great. But she possesses a common trait among ten-year-olds. She forgot to tell me we had to make cupcakes for a school project until the very last minute. We were up late baking."

My brow furrows. "Why not just go out and buy the cupcakes?"

Ginny recoils. "I'd be shunned."

"For real?"

"It's completely verboten. You can't bring in store-bought cupcakes when the class is asked to bake."

"Ah, that makes sense and fortunately, I have the solution. Next time, ask me."

She stares at me incredulously. "Why?"

The answer is easy, so easy. "Because I'll help you bake. You can call me anytime."

"But . . . you're twenty-five," she sputters, even though age has nothing to do with whether I, or anyone, can bake.

And that's when I know. That's when I fully understand this woman. Our age difference worries her. I smile. "I get you, Ginny."

"What do you get?"

I lean closer, so close I can smell honeysuckle and it's fantastic. "You think I'm too young for you. I'll have you know I'm a mature twenty-five, and I can bake my ass off."

She sighs heavily. "And I'm an old thirty-five. You know that, right?"

I shake my head. "Doesn't bother me. I don't even think about the age difference. You shouldn't either."

"I shouldn't think about how young you are?"

"Only to think about how much energy my youth gives me in many areas."

Her lips curve up. "Is that so?"

"That is *so* so."

I can sense her bending as we return to the clue, but

before we can tackle it, my teammate Leo spots a pink backpack left in the park. After a quick debate, we decide, obvs, to return it to the kid.

I grab it, and run like the cheetah I am to return it to the kid who owns it.

When I return, barely breaking a sweat from my run, I swear Ginny's looking at me in a whole new way.

She sets a hand on my arm. "That was amazing what you did, and I don't mean your stamina."

"I'm the full package, Ginny."

"Maybe you are."

And now I feel like I'm walking on sunshine.

* * *

The next day, she's not resistant at all. She's the other Ginny, the flirty one.

But she's also the *open* one.

Because as we debate where the next clue will take us, and I pray it won't be Jersey, she laughs, I nudge her, and it feels like we're all good.

Like we're in this burgeoning thing together.

After we solve the clue, and return to Central Park, we discuss important matters like pizza.

"You're really telling me you'd just lift your pizza?" I mime eating a slice, flat as a board.

"That's how we do it down under," she says with a cute little shrug.

"And I don't fold it when I visit my grandparents in Mexico City," I say. "But we're New Yorkers now. We gotta fold it. That's how we do it here."

She laughs, and smiles, and all her resistance seems to have flown out the window. "I assure you, the lift works just fine for a slice."

But just to be sure that the hurdles are gone, I seize my chance: "Let me prove the fold is better. I'll take you out to get pizza and prove it."

She nibbles on the corner of her lips. "Fine. You can prove it."

I thrust my arm in the air. "It's a date. It's a date, right?"

She grabs me by the shirt collar, looks me square in the eyes, and says in that accent that kills me, "It better be a date."

Then she brushes a kiss to my lips, and I'm over and out.

Wait.

Make that done for when she lets go, and says, "You're mine and I'm not letting you go."

There is no way I'm ever letting her get away.

A few months later, I ask her to marry me and she says yes.

The lesson? Persistence pays off.

Love is a marathon, and you have to run every mile. You have to run every mile every damn day.

And since optimism is my strong suit, I'm always up for the marathon of love.

For more on Noah and Ginny's romance, read the companion novel *Birthday Suit* and experience Lulu and Leo's love story too!

For a sneak preview of my next release, INSTANT GRATIFICATION, read on! INSTANT GRATIFICATION is a sexy friends-to-lovers, best friend's sister, fake date

romantic comedy and you can order it on all retailers!

Prologue
Jason

When you've had to tell as many "how we got together" stories as I have, you get a fair idea of the range of things a man will do to impress a woman, from thoughtful to absurd to downright unbelievable.

For starters, *bro*, did you really read *Fifty Shades of Grey*?

But that's only number one on the menu of items guys will pick and choose from in an effort to elicit flutters from a new lady.

I know men who claim to love *Pride and Prejudice*. Even go so far as to say they've read the book. And maybe we do get that desperate to see what women see in Mr. Fucking Darcy other than an English accent. Which I have, by the way, but I still don't understand the deal with Colin Firth any more than the next bloke.

I've met fellows who swear they don't like football of any variety—American or proper—to reassure a lady she'll never be a widow to the footie. Or they'll turn off a match on the TV with so much drama you'd think they were giving up a kidney.

Or a man's résumé will become suspiciously plump with female-friendly hobbies. Show me a single man in a yoga class, and I'll show you a lad who's trying to score major points with the fairer sex.

The next thing he knows, he's shaving his chest,

shaving his toes, and shaving his balls. Which must mean he's serious about her because that shit hurts.

When it comes to manscaping, I think a trim here or there can go a long way, but go too far and you'll look like a porpoise. And what woman wants to roll around in the sheets with Flipper?

But by far the worst case I ever saw was a guy who swore to his sweetheart that he loved Ed Sheeran's music. Even followed Ed's Twitter feed and read reviews so he could convincingly wax on about the ginger phenom. (The fella even planned to tell his bride that he wanted "Shape Of You" to be their wedding song. I put my foot down. Go with "Castle on the Hill." "Shape of You" is too obvious, and women can see through that lie.)

As happy as I am that it worked out for these gents, especially after they pay my invoice as a specialty wedding service provider, it seems like a lot of work to keep up with all that—retweets, nether-region mainte-nance, or the pointless hell of football abstinence.

I understand why men want to show off for women. Women are like sunshine and whiskey, lilies and diamonds. They're sex and desire and everything good in the universe. They're lovelier to gaze at than a priceless work of art. Hell, women are better than football, better than pints of ale, better than the Rolling Stones and occasionally even the Beatles, though I will deny that blasphemy even under torture.

Women make a man's merry-go-round keep turning, make life worth living. And they deserve to be annoyed if a guy who swore he hated football has a drawer full of Manchester United souvenirs.

There's a fine line between putting your best foot forward and shooting yourself in it, and it's my job to help the lead-footed of the world win women without losing them.

Damn shame, then, that the one woman I'd really like to impress is off-limits.

With good reason. With a long list of good reasons, in fact.

So off-limits is how she'll have to stay, even when I learn she desperately needs my specialized knowledge to impress a new investor.

But wouldn't you know—I need something from her too.

Badly.

That can only mean it's time to impress the hell out of *myself* by resisting every single temptation to step out of the friend zone with her.

Chapter One

Her legs wrap around my waist, firm and tight. Her heels make a vise grip, tugging me closer between her thighs.

It's the perfect position for countless naughty things. The possibilities are as vast as my filthy imagination is wide, and my imagination has won blue ribbons for its width.

Its depth too.

And its length.

Yes, it's an award-winning dirty zone between my ears.

But down here? In real life? The breath rushes from my lungs as she squeezes.

Holy hell.

I. Can't. Move.

I can barely breathe.

Truly Goodman has me pinned on the mat. She's ferocious and strong, and there's literally nothing I can do to escape her clutches.

"Nice work, Truly and Jason! That's how you neutralize a bigger, stronger opponent. With a back mount combined with a choke hold." The praise comes from the instructor.

Well, Truly's definitely neutralized any chance I'll be turned on in jujitsu class again, that's for sure. The instructor gives the go-ahead for my opponent to relinquish her hold on me, and I'm both immensely saddened that the brunette unlocks her legs from my waist and also incredibly grateful I'm not about to die in the middle of this demo of a powerful grappling move.

Truly breathes hard as she heads to the water fountain in the corner of the studio and takes a long, thirsty gulp.

Water, yes. That's a brilliant idea. I follow her to the oasis. "Have you registered those hands as lethal weapons, Truly? While you're at it, license those legs too."

She turns around, eyes me up and down, then wipes her hand across her mouth. "And yet you made it out alive. No worse for the wear."

I glance down at my frame, considering her assessment. "We can have a go again if you're interested in trying to cut off all the circulation in my body. I think you achieved a ninety percent shutdown, so why not go for broke?"

She pats my chest. "I'm always happy to take you down in class if you think your pride can take it. How much ego did that cut off?"

Scoffing, I answer, "Nothing I can't spare, given its size."

"Glad to see you're not suffering from ego shrinkage." She laughs, then nudges my elbow. "Thanks for being such a good sport. I'm going to take a quick shower since I need to head to work for a meeting. Are you going that way?"

I weigh whether to leave now, or loiter a bit and join her on her walk to Gin Joint.

Who am I kidding? Those scales will always have a Truly-shaped thumb on them. "Is fifteen minutes good for you?"

"Make it ten."

True to form, she's ready quickly, looking fresh-faced and sexy as sin in a short, painted-on skirt and a black tank top. God, I fucking love summer. It's the greatest season ever invented by man. I mean God. God invented summer, obviously. Man just invented the clothes that go with it.

"So, we've established you can take any man, woman, or three-headed beast down in a dark alley," I say once we leave the studio.

"That was my goal when I started training a few years ago. But don't sell me short. Four-headed beasts are now on my takedown list too."

"How about grizzly bears? Or, say, an anaconda?"

"Been there, done that. But listen." We stop at a light, and she glances at me then takes a breath. Her tone turns more serious. "You don't go easy on me in class, do you?"

I scoff and shoot her a *you've got to be kidding* stare. "Wait. You think I was going easy on you?"

She holds up her palms. "Just making sure you're not

one of *those* guys who thinks he has to soften things for a woman."

"There's nothing *soft* about me." I take a beat. "As you well know."

She rolls her eyes. She does that to me a lot, but I won't say I don't deserve it. "That's not what I'm saying."

"But it's spot-on true. I'd never go easy just because you're a woman." I wiggle an eyebrow. "But let's talk more about how hard you want me to be. Would you like me, for instance, somewhat harder, much harder, or *oh my God, that's so hard* harder?"

"Oh yes, please. The latter."

With a straight face, I answer, "Done. Consider it done."

"And I'm glad you don't treat me any differently because I have girl parts. I want to be tough-as-nails in this martial art."

I rub my ear. "Sorry I didn't hear anything you said after 'girl parts.' Everything else sounded like *Take me home, Jason, and make me scream your name.* Did I get that right?"

"Sure. That's exactly what I said." She laughs as we turn the corner, heading down a tree-lined block in the heart of Chelsea. "You're relentless, aren't you?"

"Yes. Not a bit of relent when it comes to some things. And along those lines," I say, stroking my chin, "that position we tried in class—just wondering if it made you think of any other interesting positions."

"Hmm." She screws up the corner of her lips, as if considering. "Nope. Can't say it did."

"None at all? Wrapping your legs around me didn't trigger any memory?"

We reach Gin Joint, the speakeasy-style bar she owns,

though to call it a bar would do it a disservice. It's an establishment with a full lounge, 1920s-style decor, and regular entertainment, including lounge singers. Her brother—my best friend—is one of those singers, and he helps draw crowds. Gin Joint has scored a place on more than one list of coolest theme bars in the city.

She stares at the sky, still bright even as the sun makes its trip toward the edge of the horizon. "I keep drawing a blank."

"Want me to give you more hints, or just spell it out for you? Things you said. I mean, things you screamed."

She stares at me for a beat. "We had an agreement. That all stays in the vault."

"But sometimes it's fun to revisit memories in the vault, isn't it?"

Laughing, she shakes her head. "Yes, but that's not the deal we made."

I know, but what can I say? I love the chase even if it'll never go anywhere, just for the sake of it. "So you do admit you enjoy taking a trip down dirty memory lane?"

"You do realize that can't happen again?" But a naughty glint crosses her pretty blue eyes. Ah, perhaps the memory is never far from the surface for her either.

I zip my lips, but then instantly unzip them. "I'm just saying." I drop my voice to a whisper. "Three times."

"*Jason.*"

I hold up my hands in surrender. "Fine, fine. Pretend you don't remember every detail in triplicate."

"I don't. I don't remember a single one."

"And I die yet again." I'm about to turn around when my mind snags on something she said earlier. "Who's your meeting with? A supplier?"

A grin seems to tug at her lips. "A restaurant and bar investor Charlotte hooked me up with. She's such a great bestie. Anyway, we're going to talk about expanding my brand. I pitched him on a new concept bar I want to start."

"You're going to be the queen of Manhattan nightlife. I'll say I knew you when."

"And you're the king of gentlemen," she says, a nod to the work I've done to establish myself as an expert on all the things a modern gentleman should know. "Are you writing a column tonight? Working on a new podcast?"

I look at my watch. "Actually, I'm meeting up with Nora, and I need to get going. She won't want to be kept waiting."

She stiffens, her hand freezing around the key in the lock. Her brow furrows as she turns to meet my gaze, her blue eyes inquisitive. "Nora?"

Do I detect a lovely note of jealousy in her voice? That may be one of the most glorious sounds I've ever heard coming from Truly Goodman's mouth.

"Who's Nora?" she asks before I can answer. "You've never mentioned a Nora."

She mentioned Nora's name three times. If that isn't a *third time's a charm* moment, I don't know what is. I decide to have fun with her. "She's my date to the wedding I'm working this coming weekend."

"Oh." It comes out heavily. "I thought you did those solo."

"Sometimes I do. Sometimes I don't." I drop a kiss to Truly's cheek, catching a faint whiff of her freshly scrubbed scent. I say goodbye and let her chew on the idea of me on a date.

Here's the thing: Truly has made it abundantly clear where we stand, and she's 100 percent right that we can't go there again—she's my best friend's sister, and she's also my very good friend.

Yet I can't help thinking about the other things she made abundantly clear one particular night earlier this year. Like how much she liked being underneath me, how much she liked being on top of me, and how much she liked me bending her over the bed.

I'm not going to say I haven't gotten her out of my mind, but I absolutely fucking haven't gotten her out of my mind. Trouble is, there are so many reasons this wouldn't work standing between us. Reasons that aren't going to change. Her reasons, and all of mine too.

So I flirt, and she hate-flirts back, a pretending-she-doesn't-like-it type of flirting. That's all we are, flirters and hate-flirters, and that's all we will ever be.

INSTANT GRATIFICATION is available to order it on all retailers!

ALSO BY LAUREN BLAKELY

FULL PACKAGE, the #1 New York Times Bestselling
romantic comedy!

BIG ROCK, the hit New York Times Bestselling standalone
romantic comedy!

MISTER O, also a New York Times Bestselling standalone
romantic comedy!

WELL HUNG, a New York Times Bestselling standalone
romantic comedy!

JOY RIDE, a USA Today Bestselling standalone romantic
comedy!

HARD WOOD, a USA Today Bestselling standalone
romantic comedy!

THE SEXY ONE, a New York Times Bestselling bestselling
standalone romance!

THE HOT ONE, a USA Today Bestselling bestselling
standalone romance!

THE KNOCKED UP PLAN, a multi-week USA Today and
Amazon Charts Bestselling bestselling standalone romance!

MOST VALUABLE PLAYBOY, a sexy multi-week USA
Today Bestselling sports romance! And its companion sports
romance, MOST LIKELY TO SCORE!

THE V CARD, a USA Today Bestselling sinfully sexy romantic comedy!

WANDERLUST, a USA Today Bestselling contemporary romance!

COME AS YOU ARE, a Wall Street Journal and multi-week USA Today Bestselling contemporary romance!

PART-TIME LOVER, a multi-week USA Today Bestselling contemporary romance!

UNBREAK MY HEART, an emotional second chance USA Today Bestselling contemporary romance!

BEST LAID PLANS, a sexy friends-to-lovers USA Today Bestselling romance!

The Heartbreakers! The USA Today and WSJ Bestselling rock star series of standalone!

The New York Times and USA Today

Bestselling Seductive Nights series including

Night After Night, *After This Night*,

and *One More Night*

And the two standalone

romance novels in the Joy Delivered Duet, *Nights With Him* and Forbidden Nights, both New York Times and USA Today Bestsellers!

Sweet Sinful Nights, Sinful Desire, Sinful Longing and Sinful Love, the complete New York Times Bestselling high-heat romantic suspense series that spins off from Seductive Nights!

Playing With Her Heart, a

USA Today bestseller, and a sexy Seductive Nights spin-off standalone! (Davis and Jill's romance)

21 Stolen Kisses, the USA Today Bestselling forbidden new adult romance!

Caught Up In Us, a New York Times and

USA Today Bestseller! (Kat and Bryan's romance!)

Pretending He's Mine, a Barnes & Noble and

iBooks Bestseller! (Reeve & Sutton's romance)

My USA Today bestselling

No Regrets series that includes

The Thrill of It

(Meet Harley and Trey)

and its sequel

Every Second With You

My New York Times and USA Today

Bestselling Fighting Fire series that includes

Burn For Me

(Smith and Jamie's romance!)

Melt for Him

(Megan and Becker's romance!)

and *Consumed by You*

(Travis and Cara's romance!)

The Sapphire Affair series...

The Sapphire Affair

The Sapphire Heist

Out of Bounds

A New York Times Bestselling sexy sports romance

The Only One

A second chance love story!

Stud Finder

A sexy, flirty romance!

CONTACT

I love hearing from readers! You can find me on Twitter at LaurenBlakely3, Instagram at LaurenBlakelyBooks, Facebook at LaurenBlakelyBooks, or online at LaurenBlakely.com. You can also email me at laurenblakelybooks@gmail.com